MYSTERIES IN OUR NATIONAL PARKS

MYSTERY
#10

RIES
ONAL PARKS

OUT OF THE DEEP

GLORIA SKURZYNSKI AND ALANE FERGUSON

For Stephanie Alm,
a rising star

Text copyright © 2002 Gloria Skurzynski and Alane Ferguson
Cover illustration copyright © 2002 Loren Long

Map by Carl Mehler, Director of Maps
Map research and production by Joseph F. Ochlak
and Martin S. Walz

Humpback whale art by Joan Wolbier

This is a work of fiction. Any resemblance to living persons or events other than descriptions of natural phenomena is purely coincidental.

Library of Congress Cataloging-in-Publication Data

Skurzynski, Gloria.
  Out of the deep / by Gloria Skurzynski and Alane Ferguson.
    p. cm.—(Mysteries in our national parks ; #10)
  Summary: Jack, Ashley, and their unreliable new foster sister set out to solve the mystery of why whales are beaching themselves at Acadia National Park.
    ISBN 0-7922-8230-2 (hc.) ISBN 0-7922-8231-0 (pbk.)
    [1. Whales—Fiction. 2. Acadia National Park (Me.)—Fiction. 3. Foster home care—Fiction. 4. National parks and reserves—Fiction. 5. Mystery and detective stories.]
    I. Ferguson, Alane. II. Title. III. Series.
  PZ7.S6287 Ou 2002
  [Fic]--dc21
                            2002005547

Printed in the United States of America

ACKNOWLEDGMENTS

The authors want to thank the following people for their wonderful help. At Acadia National Park: David A. Manski, Biologist and Chief of Resources Management; David Buccello, Chief Park Ranger; Deborah Wade, Interpretive Ranger. At Allied Whale, we're extremely grateful to Sean Todd, Senior Researcher. Sean is also Professor of Science Resource at College of the Atlantic. Many thanks also to Rosemary Seton, Whale Biologist, Director of Stranding Response Program. We're grateful to District Court Judge Kevin Sidel for his suggestions and to GenAnn Keller, Librarian. Very special appreciation goes to Vicki Lockard, editor of *Canku Ota (Many Paths)*, an online newsletter celebrating Native America, for granting us permission to use the legend about the Great Spirit and the bowhead whale.
Visit *Canku Ota* at http://www.turtletrack.org/

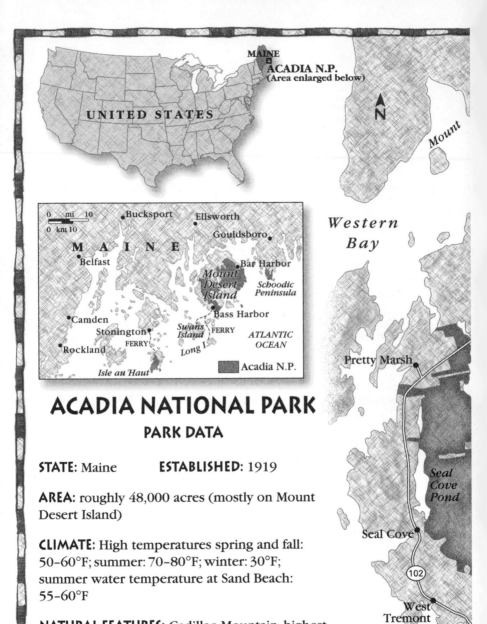

UNITED STATES

MAINE
□ ACADIA N.P.
(Area enlarged below)

N

Mount

Western Bay

MAINE

0 mi 10
0 km 10

•Bucksport   Ellsworth
              Gouldsboro•

•Belfast

Mount Desert Island

•Bar Harbor
Schoodic Peninsula

•Camden

•Bass Harbor

Stonington•   Swans Island FERRY ATLANTIC OCEAN
FERRY
•Rockland   Long I.

Isle au Haut

Acadia N.P.

Pretty Marsh•

Seal Cove Pond

Seal Cove•

102

West Tremont•

ACADIA NATIONAL PARK
PARK DATA

STATE: Maine   **ESTABLISHED:** 1919

AREA: roughly 48,000 acres (mostly on Mount Desert Island)

CLIMATE: High temperatures spring and fall: 50-60°F; summer: 70-80°F; winter: 30°F; summer water temperature at Sand Beach: 55-60°F

NATURAL FEATURES: Cadillac Mountain, highest peak on the Atlantic coast of the United States; Somes Sound, only fjord on the country's East Coast; multitudes of rocky tidal pools; more than 300 species of birds (especially shore and water varieties) and 40 species of mammals, including seals, porpoises, and whales

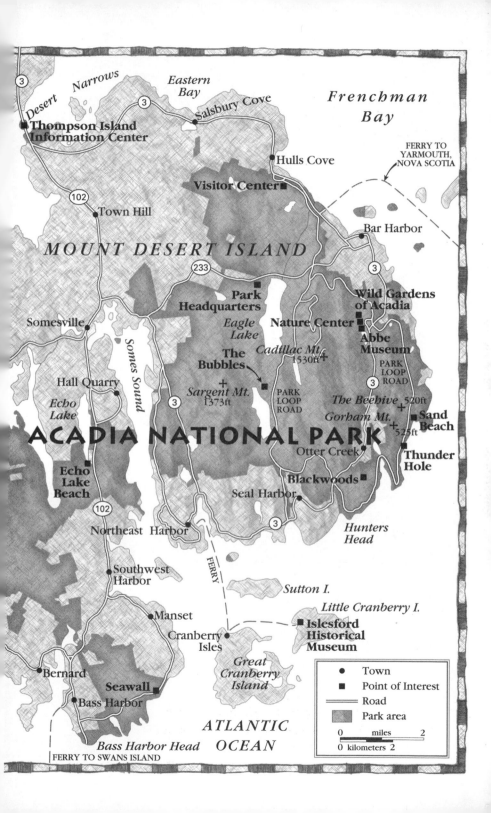

"Of course I know what's at stake," the man said gruffly, pressing the receiver against his ear. "Millions. A huge international deal. Don't worry, I won't screw up. I'll do whatever it takes. You know that."

He took a drag from his cigarette and looked around to make sure his conversation had gone unnoticed. Through the haze, he saw a couple huddled over a small table, while a grizzled man stared vacantly into his glass.

It was then that he noticed the top of a head rising from a nearby booth and two round eyes staring at him. Anger surged through him. What was a kid doing in a place like this? How much had she heard?

"Something just came up. I'll call you back," he said, slamming the pay phone into its cradle. He couldn't let some kid ruin his plan. Not now—not when they were about to cash in!

He turned quickly to make his way toward the girl. Whatever it takes, he told himself. Whatever it takes....

CHAPTER ONE

When Jack saw his mother's face, he knew the news on the other end of the phone was bad.

"Two more are *dead?*" Olivia cried into the receiver. Squeezing her eyes shut, she let out a long sigh. "This is nothing short of bizarre. I truly don't understand why they're dying this way. Where did you find the bodies? Uh-huh," she nodded, peering at a map she'd laid out on her desk, tracing it lightly with her fingertip. "Yes, I can see where that is—right at the edge of the peninsula. How badly decomposed?" Another pause, and then, "I'm sure that will make your job harder. The stench can be overpowering."

"What's up?" Jack's 11-year-old sister, Ashley, asked as she walked into the Landons' study. Their newest temporary foster child, Bindy Callister, trailed behind, a bowl of popcorn perched on her round hip. Munching noisily, she shoveled another fistful into her mouth, her cheeks bulging out like a chipmunk's. Although Bindy had been at the Landons' home for only three days, she already knew where all the food was kept and didn't seem the least bit shy about foraging through the cupboards, helping herself to whatever she found. The strangest foster kid we've ever taken in, Jack decided the day Bindy arrived.

It wasn't about the way she looked, although that had been odd enough. Bindy's tie-dyed T-shirt was wildly bright, with fluorescent swirls that splashed across her in neon constellations. Mousy brown hair had been pulled into a limp ponytail, and her too-tight jeans looked as though they'd fused onto her skin. Loud and boisterous, Bindy seemed to think she knew something about absolutely everything. When Ms. Lopez, the social worker, tried to speak, Bindy talked right over her, waving her arms as though she were on stage.

"Be patient with her," Jack's father, Steven, had told him later. "I know she can be a bit—overpowering—but she's been through a lot."

"'Cause her own parents don't want her," Ashley told Jack. "I heard Ms. Lopez tell Mom about it."

"Please don't say anything about that to Bindy!" Steven urged.

"Oh, I won't. It's just really sad. I don't know what I'd do if you and Mom didn't want *me*."

Now, as Bindy settled into a chair next to Jack, he tried to imagine what it would be like to be 14 years old and dumped into a foster home, waiting to hear what the judge ruled about your life. How would it be to have your family reject you? How would it be to have your whole future decided by someone you'd never even met before? No matter how annoying she was, Jack knew he'd have to give Bindy some space. It was the least he could do.

"Ashley, sit there," Bindy directed, pointing to a spot on the floor. "I get the chair because I'm older than you. Age before beauty!"

Ashley shot Jack a look, shrugged her shoulders, then dropped onto the carpet.

"OK. But we have to be quiet, Bindy," Ashley whispered. "Mom's on the phone."

Though Olivia Landon normally worked at the Elk Refuge at Jackson Hole, she'd converted a corner room into a home office. The large oak desk was piled high with papers stacked into a double helix. A tall coffee mug and a glass of water sat next to the computer keyboard, something their father said was dangerous, but Olivia insisted she was careful enough to handle things in her own space. Books wrapped in every color of the rainbow filled an oversize bookshelf, all of them bearing scientific titles that twisted Jack's tongue when he tried to read them out loud. The pale blue walls had been peppered with pictures of every kind of wildlife, from soaring eagles to bright-eyed foxes to coiled snakes, all photographed by their father, who dreamed of becoming a full-time photographer. Jack loved the clutter of it all. "Ideas ferment in here," Olivia always told them.

"So there's no sign of disease?" she was asking into the phone. She twisted her chair from side to side, paused, then asked, "When will the results be in?"

As Bindy noisily sucked the butter off each finger, Jack felt his teeth clench, but he willed himself to be patient. It sounded as though there might be bigger problems than an annoying foster kid.

"Hey, Jack-o, you want some popcorn?" Bindy asked, extending the bowl in his direction. "I made it the real way, with a pan and oil and real butter instead of that imitation-powder-microwave junk—"

He shook his head. *"Shhhh.* Mom's talking to a biologist at Acadia National Park. They found more bodies on the beach, which brings the total to 12."

"Twelve *people?* No way!" Bindy bellowed, slapping a thick thigh.

"Don't be stupid," Jack hissed. "A whale and some seals and stuff from the ocean. They've washed up dead, and the park people can't figure out why. Nothing quite like this has ever happened before. Try to be quiet, Bindy. My mom's talking, and I want to listen."

"Can you cut off the heads and put them on ice?" he heard his mother ask. Nodding tersely, she scratched notes on a yellow pad. Her reading glasses rested on her thin nose like half-moons, while her hair swirled to her shoulders in dark, smoky curls. Olivia, a wildlife veterinarian, was frequently called in by the parks to solve animal mysteries. There was a good possibility that she'd now be asked to Acadia National Park in Maine, about as far as you could go from their home in Jackson Hole, Wyoming, and still be in the continental United States. And maybe, Jack hoped, the rest of them would get to go, too. He'd never been to Maine.

Sighing, Olivia said, "It's a big job, but you'll need to cut off the whale's head and cool it down fast. Decomposition hides details. Heads can yield valuable clues."

Wrinkling her nose, Bindy cried, "Cutting off heads? That's so gross."

Ashley placed her finger to her lips. *"Shhhh."*

"So, who's Acadia?" Bindy asked Jack, not bothering to keep her voice low.

"Acadia is a park," he answered softly.

Olivia gave the three of them a look and extended her hand in a signal that meant "be quiet or get out." Flipping the page, she scrawled more notes.

"I still don't get it," Bindy pressed. "Why are the people in Acadia calling your mom? She's a vet in Jackson Hole. Doesn't she just deal with elk and other four-footed creatures?"

"Mom knows all about whales. She did a whole seminar on them when she was at College of the Atlantic," Ashley whispered. "Now hush—"

It was too late. "Excuse me, Sean. I'm sorry to inter-rupt, but my kids are chattering and I can't hear a word you're saying." Olivia covered the mouthpiece of the phone and waved them away. "You kids go outside for awhile. Better yet, start packing. Something's really wrong in Maine, and I need to get out there fast. We'll all go."

"Me too?" Bindy asked, wide-eyed.

"You too. We're going to Acadia!"

#

To Jack, it seemed that Bindy never stopped blabbing the whole trip. Luckily, the airlines provided earphones that could be plugged in to recorded music. Jack turned the volume as loud as he could, trying to drown out Bindy. The only time she kept silent was when she munched on the pretzels the flight attendants brought. Bindy never settled for one bag of pretzels; she always demanded three or four.

For just a little while, when they reached their motel, Bindy stayed silent. She stood on the little deck outside the room she was to share with Ashley, awestruck at the beautiful Atlantic Ocean. Gulls swooped down into the waves, picking up shellfish and dropping them onto the rocks on the beach—when the shells broke open, the gulls feasted on the critters inside.

A long wooden pier stretched from the shore, reaching like a bony finger about 60 feet into the ocean. It looked rickety, as though its support pilings had been eroded by decades of salt water. Halfway along its length there was a No Trespassing sign hanging from a chain that stretched between two posts. Except for one small rowboat near the shore, no other boats were tied to the pier.

"This is my first look at the Atlantic," Bindy murmured. "It looks greener than the Pacific."

"You've seen the Pacific?" Ashley asked.

"I used to live in California," she answered. "In Hollywood, actually."

Yeah, sure, Jack thought. In Hollywood, with movie stars, no doubt. He'd had enough of Bindy. The deck outside the girls' room was connected to the deck outside his parents' room, where Jack would be sleeping on a cot. With one hand on the banister, Jack vaulted over the railing onto his parents' deck. Then he felt like a fool, because the sliding door to his parents' room was locked. He was stuck out there, while the girls laughed at him.

Even though he'd been trying to avoid Bindy, later that evening Jack found himself knocking on the girls' door. He'd had enough of watching waves lap the shore, and his parents weren't being much company right then.

"Mom's reading a bunch of research papers about whales and Dad's going through his camera stuff, so I came to see what you guys are doing," he told Ashley when she opened the door.

"Not much. We're just flipping around the different channels." With her arm straight out, Ashley clicked the channel changer button on the remote control again and again. Bindy had spread herself on one of the queen-size beds with a book propped under her chin. She didn't bother to look up.

Suddenly Ashley yelled, "Hey wait! Look there—it's one of my favorite movies. *Melissa's Dream.*"

"You've already seen that about ten times," Jack told her, wrestling her for the remote. "You don't need to watch it again."

Ashley struggled to keep the channel changer out of Jack's reach, but his arms were longer than hers. "Jack! The movie's almost over anyway—just let me finish watching it 'cause the end's the best part."

Lifting the changer so high that Ashley couldn't reach it—considering that Jack was a good head taller than his puny little sister—he said, "OK, we'll let Bindy decide. Bindy, do you want to watch the end of this dumb movie or...."

"It's not dumb," Bindy answered. "I was in that movie."

There she goes again, Jack thought. "You mean you were *into* the movie," he said sarcastically. "Like if you go, 'I'm really into stock-car racing.' Or 'I'm really into extreme sports.' Or 'I'm really into potato chips.'"

Bindy shook her head. "I mean I was *in* the movie. I acted in it. I didn't have the leading role, but I was the cute little girl next door."

Staring at the screen, Ashley asked, "You mean *Amanda?* That was *you?* No way."

"Amanda's a redhead," Jack protested.

Scornfully, Bindy slapped her book onto her bed. "Well, duh! You've heard of hair dye, haven't you? I told the set's hairdresser not to make me so red, but she wouldn't listen because she said red was what the script called for, so red I would be. I told her it made me look like a pumpkin head. She got all mad when I said that, and then told me I didn't know anything about the business, and the only words I should speak in her presence were the lines from my script. What a grouch!" Pointing a ring-clad finger, Bindy said, "See, there I am—right there. I just walked into Melissa's kitchen. That's me."

Jack studied the girl on the small screen. If he squinted, maybe that girl did look a little bit like Bindy, but she was a lot younger and she was—thin!

"Oh, come on. You're just teasing...," Ashley began.

"No. It's me. I swear!" Flopping onto her stomach, Bindy crossed her ankles and propped her chin in her hand. Then, amazingly, she began to recite the lines at the same time the girl in the movie was saying them. Word for word, without hesitation, her lips moved in perfect sync with the dialogue on the screen. Even if she was faking it, Jack had to give her credit for a good memory.

When Bindy finished, she shot them a triumphant look. Ashley stared at her. "So that really *was* you!"

"Of course," Bindy said matter-of-factly. "I don't lie. OK, now it's over. Here come the credits. There's my name—Belinda Taylor—that's me."

"But your name's Bindy Callister," Jack broke in.

Rolling her eyes, Bindy sighed loudly. "Bindy is short for Belinda. And my name used to be Taylor until I was adopted. Before my real mother died."

"Oh," Ashley murmured. "I'm sorry...."

"Yeah, well, it was a long time ago, and I don't like to talk about it." Jerking her fingers through her thin hair, Bindy seemed to shift gears. "So anyway, I acted in seven TV commercials and one sitcom, and I had parts in two movies. The first movie was just a small part, but in *Melissa's Dream* my role was a lot bigger."

"Wow!" Ashley blurted. "That is way cool. Tell us about it. Tell us everything. Did you meet famous stars? What were they—"

Throwing up her hand like a traffic cop, Bindy demanded, "Wait! First things first. Is there anything to eat in this room? 'Cause I'm starved. If I'm going to do any talking, I need something to eat. And a can of something to drink—anything but diet. I hate diet soda."

"There's a candy machine at the end of the hall," Jack told her. "I have some change."

"So get me two Butterfingers and a can of orange soda," Bindy ordered. "Thanks, Jack-o. You're a real pal."

CHAPTER TWO

Sheesh! She was so bossy! Jack hurried down the hall to the candy machine, halfway eager to hear Bindy's story, but three-fourths of the way doubting that whatever she told them would be true. After all, Bindy was a known liar.

The evening Bindy had arrived at the Landon home, Jack had overheard his parents talking about the reason she'd been placed into temporary foster care. Olivia and Steven were at the kitchen table in terrycloth robes, sipping mugs of hot tea, their voices barely above whispers as they discussed Bindy's situation. Jack had hung back in the hallway, just until they were finished talking. It wasn't exactly eavesdropping, he'd told himself. He just didn't want to interrupt.

"...Bindy's brother Cole," Olivia was telling Steven. "According to Ms. Lopez, the tension between Bindy and Cole goes way back. Apparently he's some kind of a football star."

"More like a superstar," Steven countered. "Ms. Lopez told me Cole has already been offered full scholarships from colleges all around the country."

"Did you know that after Bindy's accusation, the football coach and his teachers all wrote letters of support for Cole, saying he was an honest and decent kid who couldn't possibly do such a thing? Ms. Lopez said no one came forward to defend Bindy."

When he craned his neck ever so slightly, Jack could catch a glimpse of his father. Steven shook his head and took another sip from his mug. "So, Bindy's adoptive parents believe Cole is telling the truth and Bindy is flat out lying. How sad for Bindy."

"I know. Still, it's possible she invented the whole thing, Steven. Ms. Lopez says Bindy comes up with one fantastic story after another. Even Ms. Lopez isn't sure how much of what Bindy says is true."

Steven set down his mug. "Having said that, it's still no excuse for what the parents are doing. I mean, how could anyone try to get rid of their own child, even if she's adopted?" Suddenly, his head jerked up and he looked toward where Jack was standing. "Wait a minute—*Jack!* Why are you lurking out there in the hall?"

Shuffling his feet, Jack emerged from the shadows. For the next ten minutes, his parents gave him a verbal going-over. Jack should never listen in on their conversation. They respected Jack's privacy, and he should do the same for them. They told him to keep everything he'd heard to himself because Bindy's private affairs were just that—her own private affairs. Since the social workers and the therapists didn't know what to make of Bindy's story, Jack shouldn't judge it, either. Instead he should give Bindy the benefit of the doubt. He was not to tell any of this to Ashley. Finally, if Bindy wanted to share her own story with Jack, that was fine, but he should in no way ask Bindy about her court case. Let her come to you, was how his mom had put it.

Now, when Jack returned to the girls' motel room, he found his sister working Bindy's hair into stubby braids. Smiling brightly, Bindy held out her hand for the Butterfingers.

"Here," Jack told her. "Catch!"

She caught one neatly and tore off the wrapper, then took a big bite. With her mouth full, she said, "Ashley's been asking questions about my so-called career, but I told her to wait until you got back. That way I can double my audience, ha ha." Pulling herself into a seated position, she proceeded to tell them about her life B.C.—before the Callisters.

She could hardly remember her father. He was killed in a speedboat accident off the coast of California when she was only three.

Back then, Bindy was cute—everyone said so—with nice round cheeks, big blue eyes, and curly blond hair.

Her mother signed her with a casting agent who arranged for Bindy to make a few commercials, but the jobs were few and far between. Bindy and her mother lived in a tiny apartment over a garage two blocks from Hollywood Boulevard. "Then I got my first movie," she said.

"And after that you were rich and famous," Ashley stated, believing it.

"Ha! I wish! I had about a dozen lines to say in that movie. Mostly I had to jump rope to 'Down by the river, down by the sea, Johnny broke a milk bottle, blamed it on me....' We must have shot that scene 20 times, and when I got so tired I started to cry, my mother took me on her lap and told me this was my big chance, and I had to be brave. So I kept doing it, over and over."

"How old were you?" Ashley asked.

"Seven. I didn't get the part in *Melissa's Dream* till I was nine. By then, my mother already had cancer."

Each day, Bindy said, her mother managed to take her to the studio where the movie was being filmed; each night they returned to the cramped apartment over the garage and rehearsed the script again and again until Bindy learned her lines. She had to be perfect; she couldn't lose that job, because they had no other income and no hospital insurance.

"That must have been awful for you," Ashley sympathized.

"No it wasn't, because we were a team. My mother loved me!" Bindy said fiercely. "We were always together—she stayed with me on the set every minute. It was months before *Melissa's Dream* was released in the theaters, and my mother kept getting sicker, but finally we went together to see the movie. Two days later, she died."

Jack felt his throat tighten as he thought of what Bindy had been through. If Bindy Callister—or Belinda Taylor—wasn't telling the truth, she was one fabulous actress. But she stayed dry eyed as she sat there telling them the rest of her story, which only got worse.

"So Aunt Marian came to Hollywood to take me home with her—she was my mother's sister. She'd seen *Melissa's Dream*, too, and she thought if she adopted me, she'd get a pretty, talented little girl to be part of her family, along with her handsome, smart, athletic son, Cole. A perfect Barbie to go with her perfect Ken doll. Hey, throw me that other Butterfinger, would you, Ashley?"

"So...so what happened?" Ashley whispered.

"Well, I didn't want to be part of Aunt Marian's perfect family. I hated Cole on sight, and he hated me, too. So...I ate. And the more I ate, the more upset Aunt Marian got. Twice she dragged me back to Hollywood to get me into another movie, but the casting director took one look at me and said no film needed a prepubescent girl with weight issues. That's how they talk in Hollywood." Bindy threw back her head and laughed a laugh so full of anger it made Jack feel creepy.

He wanted out of there. Reading his mother's thick books on whales would be better than hearing Bindy talk about her awful life, even if it was all made up.

#

Someone was moving around in the room. Jack opened one eye to stare at the digital clock on the lamp table. 12:35. Barely past midnight. He'd been asleep for only one uncomfortable hour, because the cot he was on felt lumpy.

Hair stood up on his arms as he watched the deep shadow glide silently across the floor. He could make out the outline of his parents in their bed, so it wasn't one of them who'd gotten up to go to the bathroom or anything. The shadowy shape, moving so soundlessly through the room, had to be an intruder. A thief! His fingers trembled as he watched the shape move closer. Should he call out and wake his parents or just keep quiet and let the thief take whatever he wanted?

His heart thumping so loudly the thief might hear it, Jack opened his other eye. Whoever the intruder was, he seemed awfully small. Then the shadowy figure bumped into Jack's cot and muttered, "Ouch!"

That was Jack's chance. He leaped up and grabbed the person, who wiggled and yelled, "Let go, you dork!"

"Ashley?"

"Who'd you think it was? Freddy Krueger?"

By then Jack was feeling pretty stupid—for the second time in the past six hours—so he grumbled, "What the heck are you doing sneaking around in the dark?"

"What's going on?" Olivia asked, turning on the bedside lamp. Her dark hair sprang from her head in wild curls. Blinking hard, she asked, "Where's Bindy?"

"That's what I came to tell you," Ashley answered calmly. "She's gone."

Steven sat upright. "Gone? Gone where?"

Plunking herself down on the end of Jack's cot, Ashley replied, "I have no idea. I heard a door close, and at first I thought it was the bathroom door and Bindy had just gone in to…you know. I was kinda sleepy, so I don't know how much time went by, but then I looked over at her bed and it was empty. I got up and looked into the bathroom, and that was empty, too."

Both Steven and Olivia were on their feet so fast it was as though they'd been shot out of a cannon. They practically dove into their jeans and then pulled sweatshirts over their heads, yanking them into place as they ran through the door that connected Ashley's room to theirs. In less than a minute they were back, looking grim.

"I'll check at the front desk," Steven said.

"It's after hours. I doubt anyone will still be there," Olivia said.

Jack suggested, "Maybe she just couldn't sleep. She could have gone out on the beach to look at the waves." Before he even spoke the last word, Steven rushed out the door. Jack listened for the clatter of his father's footsteps going from the front deck down the wooden stairs to the parking lot, then remembered that his dad had-n't bothered to put on shoes. Steven's feet were going to get awfully sore clambering barefoot over the rocky beach.

Olivia had begun to page through a phone book, muttering, "I'm calling the police."

"Don't you think you ought to wait a little while?" Jack asked her. "At least until we look around the motel. Maybe she just went for a Coke in the drink machine." Or a couple more candy bars, he thought.

Olivia slammed down the receiver, saying, "You're right. Kids, get dressed. We'll do a thorough search. *Then* I'll call the police. And grab your dad's shoes on your way out. He's going to need them."

After catching up to Steven and handing him the shoes, Olivia and Ashley left to scour the grounds of the motel while Steven and Jack walked along the shore, peering inside weathered boats and searching protruding rock formations that seemed to bubble up from the water's edge. Lights from a few distant build-ings twinkled in the darkness. Jack would have felt cheered if it hadn't been such a serious situation. Olivia's faint voice wafted to them. "Anything?"

Steven called back, "No!" Then, to Jack, he grum-bled, "This is ridiculous. Where could she be?"

Suddenly, Jack snapped his fingers. "Hey, wait a minute—did you check the pier?"

"Of course I checked the pier."

"But did you go past the No Trespassing sign? There are steps way at the end of the pier—I could see them from our balcony. Bindy might be sitting at the bottom of the steps just looking at the waves. She said she likes the Atlantic," he finished lamely.

Steven sighed and ran his fingers through his thinning blond hair. "I went to the point where the chain blocks it off. I couldn't see too well, but I called for her. Nothing. She's not there."

"Except she might not have answered you. She's really weird. Maybe she'll answer if it's me. Dad, you just keep looking around. I'll be right back."

"All right. I'll give you two minutes. Then we're going back to the motel to get help."

"Right. Two minutes!" Broken seashells crunched underfoot as Jack made his way to the pier. Tall enough for larger boats to load and unload, the pier had a row of rickety stairs that descended from the far end to the water's surface. At the halfway point, a metal chain had been strung across to prevent access, with the No Trespassing sign hanging from the links and a smaller sign reading "Enter at your own risk" beneath that. But no signs would keep Bindy out. She did what she wanted to do and went where she wanted to go.

Moving along the creaking, splintery slats, Jack called out her name into the night sky. Only the sound of waves and the groan of the wooden pier echoed back. As he squinted into the darkness, he saw what he thought was a dark shape, a deep patch of black turned toward the sea. "Hey, are you there?" Jack cried. The shape seemed to move farther away, hovering at the pier's end, then disappearing.

Glancing around quickly to see if his dad was watching, Jack easily climbed over the chain. A sudden wind whipped his face, ballooning out his shirt as though it were a shroud and rocking the pier like a trapeze. For a moment Jack wondered whether there might be any missing boards underfoot that he couldn't see in the dark. He didn't want to fall through onto the rocky beach beneath, where waves could grab him and soak him to the skin. With every motion the sun-bleached boards creaked under his feet, as the cold and insistent wind tried to push him backward. But someone was down there. It had to be Bindy.

He cupped his hands again against the wind and called out, "Is that you?" After waiting a beat, he shouted again. The boardwalk stretched into darkness. Jack could hear, rather than see, the water beneath him, rushing against the timbers before receding back to the sea. The inky night at the pier's end seemed denser now. As the shape blocked his view of whitecaps on the dark waves, Jack noticed a pale, orange glow. It illuminated the shadowy figure's head. The shape was bigger than Bindy, taller, broader in the shoulders— or was Jack being deceived by the darkness? He took another step. "Bindy?"

When the shape turned, Jack's breath sucked into his throat. This wasn't Bindy. It was a man, dressed in black, with a black wool coat that skimmed the tops of his boots. A rectangular metal box—a suitcase?—rested inches from his feet.

"What do you want?" the man growled. His knit cap had been pulled down onto his thickly featured face. A cigarette hung from his lips, the lit end dancing in the night. The light from the cigarette let Jack see the man's expression, and the look made his mouth go dry.

"I asked you a question. Are you going to answer me?" The man took a drag from the cigarette, then flicked it into water.

"I want—nothing," Jack stammered. "I'm looking for a girl. Have you seen her?"

"I dunno. What's she look like?"

"She's 14, she has light brown hair, and she's…uh…." Jack made a half-hearted gesture.

"Kind of chunky?" the man finished.

"Yes! So you saw her?"

"No, I didn't see anyone like that. I came down here for a private smoke," he answered, lighting up another cigarette. "No one indulges anymore, so I have to find places where I won't bother anyone, and no one will bother me. OK?"

"It's just that she—the girl—is missing. Have you been up here long?"

"No." Taking another drag, the man blew it between his teeth and asked, "Why?"

"I'm asking just in case maybe you saw her walking along the beach. We're really worried about her." Smoke curled toward Jack, and the smell hit him, acrid and pungent. How could anyone suck that stuff into their lungs? It was gross.

Suddenly, the heel of the man's boot struck hard on the boardwalk as he took a step forward. "Where are you staying?"

The question caught Jack off guard. "At the Seaside Motel. Up there." He gestured.

"Yeah? What's your name?"

"I—I don't think you need to know my name. Anyway, I'd better go." There was something wrong here, something Jack couldn't quite put his finger on. The man had only taken a single step toward him, and yet Jack felt his muscles tense in a "flight or fight" reaction.

He was relieved when he saw his father halfway down the beach. Steven spotted him and waved his arms in the air. "Jack!" he yelled. "I told you not to go past the chain. Come back here right now!"

The man snorted. "So it's *Jack*, is it? Well, Jack, I guess it's time for you to go. To answer your question, I didn't see anything, I didn't hear anything. And Jack— it'd be smart if you did the same."

What did *that* mean? Spinning on the toes of his

sneakers, Jack began to climb the stairs. With his back toward the man, he felt exposed, as if something might hit him between the shoulder blades at any moment. Don't be stupid, he chided himself. The man's just weird. With Bindy gone, the Landons had bigger problems. Swinging himself over the chain, he hurried along the pier to join Steven, who had a look of panic on his face.

"Dad—there's this guy up on the pier—"

"Did he see Bindy?"

"No."

"I can't find her anywhere. Let's move it. We need to look around the motel."

The four Landons checked all the halls, which were strangely empty. "What if she's gone into someone's room?" Steven worried.

Olivia groaned, " I can't even deal with that possibility. I'm calling the police right now!"

CHAPTER THREE

Jack could hear only one side of the conversation as his mother stated, "Her name is Bindy Callister. B-I-N-D-Y. Short for Belinda. Fourteen, blondish hair, a bit overweight." With her hand over the mouthpiece, she asked Ashley, "Do you know what she had on?"

Ashley shrugged. "The last time I saw her, she was wearing a sleep shirt. She was reading in bed with the light on. Then I fell asleep."

Olivia had turned all her attention to the phone again, concentrating so hard it looked like she might shoot through the phone lines, like Trinity in *The Matrix*. "Yes," she was saying. "Yes, that's right. Fourteen. She is? You do? Oh thank—We'll be right there. Uh…where is the police station? We just arrived this afternoon, and we don't know anything about Bar Harbor." Grabbing a ballpoint pen from the desk drawer, Olivia began to scribble directions. Then, slowly, she returned the phone to its cradle.

"Good news or bad news?" Steven asked.

"Both. The police have her. But they picked her up in a *bar.*"

Had Jack heard that right? "Did you say they picked her up in Bar Harbor?" he asked.

"No, I said in a bar. A place that serves alcohol. Oh, Steven," Olivia cried, reaching for his hand, "maybe we're in way over our heads with this girl. She was able to sneak out right under our noses. When I imagine what could have happened—maybe she's too much for us to handle. We've never dealt with anything like this before."

"Now calm down," he said. "Let's all pile into the car and find the police station."

That's what they did, heading onto the highway that led to Bar Harbor, since the Seaside Motel was located about five miles from the town proper. In the back seat, Ashley held a flashlight while Jack tried to follow the street map of Bar Harbor, and Olivia studied the directions she'd scribbled. The town wasn't all that big, but it had a lot of quirky little side streets that confused Jack. "I can't really tell...," he muttered. "Wait, turn here," he told his father, who was driving. After a couple more turns they found the police station, a pale brick building, squat and square and plain, as if it, like the state of Maine, would tolerate no nonsense. Lights radiated from inside the building, casting a greenish glow onto the street. What a scary place for Bindy to be! Steven must have been thinking the same thing, because he didn't even bother to parallel park. He left the car sitting with one tire on the curb and the headlights still on, as the family hurried into the station.

The first thing Jack saw when he walked in was Bindy. She sat alone on a wooden bench, elbows resting on her knees and her head in her hands. Her mousy hair had fallen forward to cover her features. When she looked up, Jack could see fear in her eyes.

A policewoman, stifling a yawn, stood up from behind her desk to approach the Landons. "Sorry to drag you folks in here in the middle of the night. I'm Officer Bartlett. Is this the girl you phoned about?"

"She's the one," Steven answered grimly.

"Officer Wilson picked her up in Smokey's Bar about an hour ago—the bar's up the hill, not too far from your motel. Anyway, the bartender had called us, saying he had a minor on his premises. He said she was a lot more underage than what he usually gets—which is, you know, 17- or 18-year-olds. That's why he didn't want to throw her out alone into the night. So we told him to just leave her there and not say or do anything until we sent an officer."

Olivia's brows knit together as she asked, "Is she being charged with a crime?"

"No. She didn't try to order any alcohol; she said she just went into the bar to use the pay phone. We could charge her with breaking curfew, but...let's just say she convinced us all that she'll never do it again. Your girl can be very persuasive."

Steven and Olivia sat down on either side of Bindy. Jack could tell that his mother was trying to keep her voice calm as she said, "That sounds pretty lame, Bindy. The pay phone? If you wanted to make a call, why didn't you just use the phone in your room?"

Squeezing her eyes tight, Bindy answered, "I didn't want Ashley to hear. It was a private call."

"To whom?" Steven demanded. "Who were you trying to call at midnight?"

"Why should I even answer? I know you won't believe me. Nobody ever believes me. Except these kind officers here. They listened."

"Try us," Steven said. It was Olivia, though, who reached out to cover Bindy's hand with her own. Maybe she'd noticed the tears welling up in the girl's eyes. Even from across the room, Jack had noticed that. Real tears? Or part of an act?

Her words came out in a rush. "I wanted to call Aunt Marian, but I never even got to use the pay phone because this jerky man was on it and he wouldn't hang up—he kept talking to someone about a boat and he was going on and on and on. I was in a booth right behind him, and I waited and waited, and then he turned and looked at me and said—" She stopped for breath, then muttered, "Forget it—it doesn't matter what he said. So I went to ask the bartender if I could use his private phone and I'd pay him for the call, but before I could, the policeman came in and arrested me."

"Why did you want to call your aunt?" Ashley broke in. "You told us she was really mean to you."

Olivia shook her head, trying to cue Ashley to keep quiet, but too late—Bindy dissolved into tears as she wailed, "Because I want to go home. When we were watching *Melissa's Dream,* I started thinking about my mom, and—and I started to miss having a family. Aunt Marian and Uncle Jim and Cole—they're the only family I've got left." Her voice quivered as she spoke, but she seemed to will herself to go on. "OK, so she loves Cole way more than me, but I can live with that. At least with them I had a home. Now I don't know what's going to happen to me. No one wants me. The only one who ever really loved me is dead."

Both Olivia and Steven put their arms around Bindy and raised her to her feet. "It's all right," they were telling her. "You're with us now. Let's get back to the motel. It's late, and we have to check on a dead whale tomorrow." To the officer, Steven said, "I guess it's all right for us to take her with us, isn't it, since she's not being charged with anything."

"You have to sign some papers," Officer Bartlett answered, "and then she can go. Technically, we could charge her with theft, but we'll let it go—at least this time."

"Theft!" Steven exclaimed.

"I needed money for the pay phone, so I borrowed a bunch of quarters off a table," Bindy cried. "I had three dollars in my pocket—I was going to put the bills back on the table to replace the quarters. Honest!" When Olivia looked skeptical, Bindy added quickly, "I just didn't have time before I was arrested."

The ride back to the motel was silent, except for Bindy's sniffles. Jack couldn't tell if she was still crying or if she was pretending. With Bindy, the actress, it was hard to separate truth from fiction. Yet her tears in the police station, when she'd sobbed that nobody wanted her, had seemed real enough.

Jack was ready to agree with his mother. Bindy Callister might be more than the Landons could handle.

#

Everyone in the rental car stayed quiet. They'd had less than five hours' sleep from the time they got back from the police station until the alarm clocks buzzed in both their motel rooms at 7:30 a.m.

That is, everyone but Bindy, who chattered just as much as usual. "...so when I found out they were shooting the movie in New Zealand, I thought maybe I could get a role as a hobbit, just to get away from my aunt. After all, kids at school kept telling me I looked like a hobbit— short and wide. One guy even asked me to take off my shoes so he could see if I had hairy feet. So I did. I took off one shoe and hit him over the head with it. Too bad it wasn't a spike heel...." And on and on.

If Bindy hadn't yapped so much, Jack could have enjoyed the scenery more. The park covered 35,000 acres of much larger Mount Desert Island, named by the French explorer Samuel de Champlain, who landed there in 1604. They hadn't reached the park boundary yet; instead, they drove on a winding two-lane road through hills bedecked with greenery—beautiful but impossible to appreciate because Bindy the Blabber showed no signs of winding down.

Finally, to shut her up, Jack asked, "Mom, what about these marine mammals that are stranding?"

Before Olivia had a chance to reply, Bindy said, "Mammals. That must be where the word 'mamma' comes from. Mammals, mamma. Mamma, mammals."

Olivia answered, "Those words aren't connected, Bindy. 'Ma' is one of the easiest sounds for a baby to make. Proud mothers tell you, 'Oh, she's so smart. She's only four months old, and she's already saying 'Mamma,' but it's only baby babble. It doesn't mean anything."

Bindy smacked her forehead and cried dramatically, "Oh dear! Another illusion smashed!"

Sheesh! Tired and cranky, Jack decided he'd had enough of Bindy's theatrics. "Will you please keep quiet long enough for my mother to answer my question about the strandings?" he demanded.

"I do talk a lot, don't I. When I was making movies—"

"*Just—shut—up!*"

"Jack!" his father warned, frowning at him in the rear view mirror—the three kids were in the back seat of the rented Ford Taurus, crowded tight because of Bindy's width.

"Sorry," Jack mumbled. "Mom, please tell us about the strandings."

His mother twisted around from the front seat to face him. "First, Jack, I don't like you being rude to Bindy. Second, I want to finish what I was explaining. The word 'mammal' comes from the Latin word—"

Oh, crud! Jack knew where the word "mammal" came from, and he knew exactly what the Latin word meant—it had to do with how female animals fed their babies. It would be so embarrassing to listen to an explanation of mammary glands while he was jammed thigh to thigh beside Bindy. "Let her look it up in the dictionary," he muttered, but his mother ignored him. He covered his ears with his hands and started making soft *na-na-na* noises inside his throat until Olivia finished her lecture, but he could still feel his cheeks growing hot.

"You are such a dork, Jack," Ashley told him, reaching across Bindy to smack him on the knee. "You just acted like you were about three years old."

For once, Bindy said nothing, but Jack could see that she looked a little embarrassed, too.

"Now about strandings," Olivia went on. "As you know, Bindy—or maybe you don't know—marine mammals like whales and dolphins and porpoises and seals live in the water, but they have to breathe air. They stay submerged for a while, then every so often they surface to take a breath. If they didn't, they'd suffocate, just as you or I would drown underwater if we couldn't breathe."

Sitting twisted around like that must have made Olivia uncomfortable, because she turned to face forward again. Since she never missed a chance to teach something to kids, she pulled down the car's sun visor and spoke into its mirror, looking at the kids' reflections while she talked.

"To answer your question about the strandings, Jack, marine mammals strand for a variety of reasons—injury or disease or harassment from humans or pollution in the water or getting tangled in nets. And if baby whales become separated from their mothers, they'll often strand because they can't find food by themselves."

Steven added, "Sometimes stranded marine mammals are already dead when they wash ashore. Other times they wash ashore first. And then they die."

"Do they always have to die? Can't anyone save them?" Ashley pleaded.

Olivia hesitated. "Seals are easiest to save; dolphins and porpoises, maybe half the time. Whales are harder to save. Very hard."

She paused then, as though she didn't know whether to get specific.

"They can be pushed back to sea, can't they?" Jack asked. "I've read about that. And then they'll make it OK, won't they? They'll live?"

Olivia was shaking her head again, more slowly this time. "Rescuers do try to haul them back into the water, and sometimes it works, especially with the smaller whales. But usually they're just too huge to move. Time is really critical when a whale is stranded. If it can't be refloated quickly...."

In a very small voice that didn't even sound like her, Bindy asked, "What happens then?"

"Well, nobody likes to see a whale die an agonizing death, its body crushed under its own weight on a beach. So they're often euthanized—put to death as humanely as possible. They're so huge, it takes massive doses of euthanizing agent."

Bindy gasped. Jack guessed she didn't know about the bad things that could happen in the animal world, the way he and Ashley did. They'd traveled with their mother and father to a number of national parks where species were in trouble, and sometimes animals died—the condors at Grand Canyon; the manatees at Everglades; the cougar at Mesa Verde that had to be put down because it had attacked a child. Nature could be brutal, yet all too often the damage to animals was caused by humans. Usually it happened because people were just careless, but other times it was because they were criminals, like the men in Glacier National Park who kidnapped bear cubs.

"I think we're here, guys," Steven announced after turning onto a side road. He swung into a parking lot and pulled up near a building marked Visitor Center Acadia National Park. "OK, everybody out!" he ordered, but even before he said it, Jack had flung open the car door to escape, glad to get some space again.

Bindy got out more slowly. From the curb, she pointed to the Visitor Center and asked, "Do they sell candy bars in there? I'm starved."

"Well, if you hadn't caused so much trouble last night," Jack snapped, "we could have had time for a real restaurant breakfast." Instead, they'd settled for oatmeal bars Olivia had brought from home.

"Everything's always my fault," Bindy muttered.

"Never mind," Steven told her. "When it's time for lunch, I'll see that you get a decent meal."

CHAPTER FOUR

The park resource manager, Greg, impressed Jack. He was tall and muscular, with thick salt-and-pepper gray hair, and he looked good in his National Park Service uniform. At every national park the Landons had visited, Jack had felt admiration for the rangers, biologists, naturalists, and law enforcement people who seemed to care so much about the jobs they were doing to preserve the best part of America—its wildlands, history, and natural beauty. He'd started to think he might like to work for the Park Service himself, after he grew up and finished college.

"My office is pretty small," Greg was apologizing, "so I thought we'd better meet here in the conference room. I didn't know there'd be so many of you Landons," he added, laughing.

"I'm not a Landon," Bindy announced, shaking

Greg's outstretched hand. "I'm Bindy Callister, a problem child the Landons are stuck with for a while."

Greg looked a little surprised, but he smiled and said, "Well, have a chair then. You can sit next to me, Bindy Callister, problem child." When he pulled out the chair, Bindy plunked onto it and grinned up at him.

The Landons seated themselves around the table, with Olivia opposite Greg. Immediately getting down to business, she said, "Just to review the facts, you had 12 marine mammals strand at Isle au Haut a week ago. All of them were dead, or died shortly after stranding, correct? There were 5 seals, including 3 mature animals and 2 pups; 6 porpoises, all mature; and one humpback whale, a mature female 40 feet long and weighing approximately 37 tons." Dropping her professional manner, Olivia exclaimed, "You must have had some job getting that body off the beach."

Greg nodded. "Even after the head was cut off and sent to Harvard Medical School for examination, that still left a lot of whale carcass to remove. Fortunately, we had a large group of volunteers helping us do the job, and the weather has been cool for May. If it had been hot and sunny, the smell would have made us all gag. It was bad enough as it was."

"Where are the other carcasses?" Steven asked.

"In an ice storage unit in Bar Harbor. We'll drive over there later, Olivia, so you can examine them."

Bindy wrinkled her nose as though the thought of examining dead animals was disgusting. She was just about to say something when Steven gave her "the look," a forbidding expression he'd perfected with his own kids. It worked on Bindy, too. She kept quiet.

"The first thing that crossed my mind was sonar testing," Olivia continued. "After that case in the Bahamas where 16 whales and a dolphin beached...."

"Olivia, refresh my memory about that case, will you?" Greg asked. "I know that acute auditory trauma and the intense pain connected with it can really mess up a whale's navigation system. Maybe you didn't hear about it, but just north of here, off the coast of Newfoundland, there were some explosions from an underwater drilling operation that could have interfered with the navigational skills of a bunch of humpback whales. They blundered into fishing nets."

Steven commented, "Getting tangled up in nets can be as bad for whales as strandings."

"Definitely. Still, in the 11 years I've been here," Greg went on, "we've had a couple of whales that were already dead come floating ashore, but we've never had anything like the *mass* stranding that happened this week. It sounds more like the case in the Bahamas."

Olivia shuffled some papers before she said, "I'll tell you what I've been able to research so far, Greg. The Bahamas stranding involved 16 whales and 1 dolphin." She went on to explain that just before the whales washed up on the beach, the U.S. Navy had been testing mid-frequency sonar in the ocean, not too far away. The stranded whales were a smaller species that weighed only about 2 tons each, so volunteers could push most of them back into the water. "But 7 of the whales died right on the beach, and none of the others have been seen since then."

"So they died, too," Ashley whispered softly. "Except they died out in the ocean."

Greg asked, "Did you read the necropsy report? I managed to get a copy of it. Biologists examined the tissue and bones around the whales' ears and found that they'd hemorrhaged."

"Right. Since whales live in a world of sound, they need their hearing for communicating with each other—and for finding their way around, locating food, and avoiding predators. In other words," she said, explaining it for Bindy's benefit, "they make sounds and listen to the sounds echoing back to them. That's how they tell where objects are in the water."

Steven added, "It's the same principle as the sonar the Navy was testing—they send out a signal and listen for its echo."

"Right. Anyway, it seemed pretty certain that the Navy's sonar testing confused the whales and caused the stranding in the Bahamas." Olivia picked up the report and waved it. "As things turned out, the necropsies—that means autopsies on animals, Bindy—proved that the sonar had done more than just confuse them, it had actually damaged the whales' ears. Three of them showed signs of bleeding in their inner ears, and one showed signs of bleeding around the brain."

"That's bad," Jack declared. "I hope the Navy stopped doing the sonar testing after that."

Greg looked a bit uncomfortable. Drumming his fingers on the tabletop, he said, "You know, I was in the military myself before I joined the Park Service. Quite often, the military has to walk a fine line between defense measures and environmental harm."

"Yeah, I read about the decision in this particular case," Steven agreed. "The Navy said it would protect marine mammals as much as possible—during peacetime. But they also said that national security comes first. And right now, since the war against terrorism began, this is no longer considered peacetime."

"Correct. And the sonar they were testing is used to detect enemy submarines," Greg added. Standing up for emphasis, he declared, "However, I am absolutely sure that the Navy has not been testing low-frequency, mid-frequency, or any range frequency of sonar in these waters this week or the week before. I personally spoke to a high-ranking officer in the Navy Department, and he assured me of this. I believe him."

"Then what?" Olivia asked. "What caused it? Has anyone performed a necropsy so far on any of the dead marine mammals?"

Greg sat down again, looking grim. "Yes. On one of the dolphins."

"And the results?" Steven asked softly.

"Hemorrhage of the inner ear."

The room was silent. *Sonar,* Jack thought.

"So the Navy lies," Bindy blurted. "Hey, everybody calls me a liar, but my little exaggerations are puny compared with this coverup!"

"Bindy!" Steven cried sharply. "That's enough."

With her forefinger, Bindy pretended she was sewing her mouth shut.

Looking angry, Olivia murmured, "Steven, why don't you take the kids for a drive around the island. Greg and I have a few things to go over, and then I want to examine the dead marine mammals. We'll meet later at the motel—you can take the kids back there after they've had a chance to see the park."

"Right." Steven had them on their feet and out of the meeting room so fast, Jack felt like he was being herded by a sheepdog.

#

Jack had jumped into the front seat of the car next to his dad. He didn't want to get stuck with Bindy, who sat in the back with Ashley. Heading south from the Visitor Center, they'd done the tour the way most tourists did—from the inside of their car. Steven drove silently, his mouth clamped in a firm line. Jack was afraid to ask him to stop so they could get out to enjoy the view.

With nothing better to do, Jack started reading the roadside signs. One said, "Wild Gardens of Acadia," but they passed that turnoff. The next read "Abbe Museum," and they passed that one, too. The next sign said "Bridge Clearance 12 feet 2 inches." With interest, Jack studied the bridge that arched above the road. Made entirely of slabs of sand-colored stone, it seemed to have been put together as intricately as a jigsaw puzzle.

He wondered if his dad was going to keep driving aimlessly, or if he had a place in mind to stop and take pictures. They'd already passed a lot of scenic spots. At last he slowed the Taurus and pulled into a small parking place. "Everybody out," he told them. "This is the place I wanted you to see."

Red spruce trees towered overhead. As they walked, Jack could smell the salty Atlantic mixed with the pungent tang of evergreen. The sound of waves crashing against rock filled him with anticipation, yet he couldn't see beyond the army of trees, which frustrated him. Jackson Hole had towering mountains, but there was something almost mystical about the ocean, and the sooner he could touch the waves, the better. Ashley, too, seemed excited. She kept dancing on ahead until she disappeared behind a bend in the trail. Jack, Steven, and Bindy trotted along behind. Silently, Jack willed Bindy to keep quiet and move faster.

"Hey—how much farther?" Bindy asked, sucking in a gulp of air.

"Not much," Steven replied. "It's just down that path."

"Good. I'm not much of a hiker, although I've played one on TV. Hah!" Bindy laughed at her own joke. "Did I ever tell you about how I did this one show where I was supposed to take a fish off a hook, but I said to the director, 'I can't do it 'cause its little fishy eyes are staring at me!' and the director told me I had to for the scene, you know, so then I go, 'Well, it's against my religion because I'm a vegan, and vegans don't touch flesh.' Technically, I wasn't actually a vegan, but my mom was, so I figured it half counted. So then the director yells to the prop guy to get a rubber fish and that's what I ended up pulling off the hook—a wet fake trout that still grossed me out, 'cause one of its glass eyes fell right into my hand. Whew! How long is this trail?"

"Just a little farther," Steven replied. "We're almost there. I wanted to take you through the back trail so you could get the full effect."

"So you might want to save your breath," Jack added.

"Hey Jack," Ashley called out, "turn around and look at that mountain."

Jack glanced behind him, then twisted to the left and the right. Puzzled, he asked, "What mountain? I don't see any mountain."

Ashley grinned. "Back home in Jackson Hole, we'd call it a bump in the road. Here, it's named The Beehive. I saw a sign."

After a minute Jack saw what Ashley was pointing to. "That?" he exclaimed. In Wyoming, the Landons lived in the shadow of the 13,770-foot-tall highest peak of the Grand Tetons. Back there, this little Maine "mountain" would hardly qualify as a molehill. "How high is it?" he asked his dad.

Steven checked his guidebook before he answered, "520 feet above sea level. And that one over there, Gorham Mountain—" He pointed. "The book says it's 525 feet high. But the really big one here on Mount Desert Island is called Cadillac Mountain. It stands all of 1,530 feet high."

"Wow!" Jack exclaimed sarcastically.

When all three Landons began to laugh, Bindy scolded,"You guys are mountain snobs. Mountains have feelings, you know."

"Oh, come on...," Jack began, but Bindy broke in with, "And I have feelings, too, like hunger. I don't suppose there are any restaurants up ahead?"

"Hello—it's a national park," Jack snapped. "There are no restaurants on the beach. Besides, how could you be all that hungry when you had five oatmeal bars less than two hours ago?"

"Sheesh, it was just a question. Chill out, Jack-o. If I get too hungry, I'll bite my nails." A beat later she added, "That was a joke, in case you didn't catch it. Besides, I can't help it if I have a healthy appetite."

"If you exercised more you'd—"

"Jack, could I talk to you for a minute?" Steven broke in.

Sighing, Jack fell back into step next to his father. Steven didn't have to say a word, since Jack already knew the drill: Be nice, be supportive, and above all, don't provoke the foster kid. But what about when the foster kid provoked him?

It took a moment for Steven to speak. A layer of pine needles muffled their footsteps, as if they were walking on blankets. The two of them swung into an easy rhythm, pulling low-hanging branches back in tandem. "You doin' OK, Son?" his father finally asked.

"Yeah," Jack shrugged. "Just tired, I guess."

"It was a late night for us all. Don't let your tiredness get the better of you, though. Understand?" When he reached out and ruffed Jack's hair, Jack managed a weak smile. It wasn't his dad's fault that they'd gotten "The Mouth" for a foster child. Well, no matter what, the one thing Jack could take comfort in was that foster kids didn't stay in the Landon home forever.

From behind, he noticed that Bindy didn't move anything like Ashley, who hopped over rocks and ducked boughs as nimbly as a deer. Bindy's gait, in contrast, seemed almost awkward, as if her round arms and legs couldn't quite swing in rhythm. It was hard to believe she had ever been in movies. Jack suddenly remembered that the girl in *Melissa's Dream* hadn't moved like that—the character named Amanda was a gymnast who could walk on a balance beam while talking to Melissa. One more clue that Bindy was faking. Could he ever believe a word out of her mouth?

Steven hitched his backpack full of camera equipment farther up on his shoulders. "Hang on, Bindy, it's just about a hundred yards more. One thing you should know—even though Sand Beach will look like it has real sand, it's actually quite different from what you'd find anywhere else in the park. You can see that on either end, Sand Beach has rocks like the rest of the shoreline of Acadia, but along the crescent—"

"Uh-uh," Bindy interrupted. "Can't get a tan on those rocks, that's for sure. You know, a tan is mandatory on the West Coast. Everyone in Hollywood keeps their skin bronzed and their teeth white, although I think their smiles look like a bunch of piano keys with lips. So fake. Plus, everyone in Hollywood has to be stick thin. Even the guys eat salad. I'm telling you, it's a weird place."

Steven nodded. "Yes, well, as I was saying, the sand on this particular beach isn't really sand. It's made up of ground-up shells that've been bashed by the waves until they turned flaky and gritty. Olivia and I came to this park when we were first married, and I found out just how different Sand Beach was. That shell dust stuck to my wet feet like a second skin, and it was all but impossible to brush off. Look," he pointed, "there are the steps that lead to the beach. I see Ashley's already found her way down."

"If there's no food, can I at least have some water?" Bindy begged. "You have some water in your backpack, don't you Mr. Landon?"

"I do. Jack, I know you're eager to get to the beach. You go on ahead while I dig out the water bottle."

Jack didn't need to be told twice. The army of spruce had broken apart to reveal a stone stairway descending to the shoreline. Bolting down the steps, he emerged onto a crescent-moon beach of pinkish beige sand that stretched the width of more than two football fields. On either end of the crescent, slabs of granite rose out of the waves, as though a race of giants had been making sand castles that suddenly turned to stone. Ashley stood at the water's edge, hugging herself as the ocean breeze whipped her hair into tight ringlets. Except for his sister, the beach was empty. The sand gave way under his feet as he walked over to join her.

"Where's Bindy?" she asked, her eyes still focused on the waves.

"Back with Dad. It'll take her a minute."

"Good. No offense, but this place needs to be enjoyed in silence. Isn't this awesome?"

Jack nodded as he soaked up the view around him. Dozens of tidal pools shimmered like liquid glass in the dim sunlight, the largest of them surrounded by angry gulls quarreling over what was left of a fish. Beyond the tide, seawater pounded huge boulders, roiling and foaming white before retreating to the sea, only to surge again.

It was the mix of colors that mesmerized Jack. The Virgin Islands had been painted with pastels; Acadia's palette was forged of grays, greens, blues, and pearl.

"I've hardly had a chance to talk to you," Ashley began. She stood unmoving, her eyes on the waves. "What do you make of Bindy?"

Jack shrugged. "I don't know. What's your opinion?"

"I'm the one asking you, Jack."

"Well, I don't know what to say. She's...different."

"It's just, last night, she—she told me some things. Do you believe all the stuff she tells you?"

He hesitated just long enough to give his answer. No. The more time he spent with Bindy, the more he was convinced that everything, from her brother to Hollywood and everything in between, had been embroidered with untruths stitched upon exaggerations so that nothing real remained. Maybe the fabric underneath was true, but that was all.

Placing his hand on his sister's elbow, he asked, "What's going on?"

"After we got back and Mom moved into our room to make sure Bindy didn't leave again," Ashley began, her words rushing on top of each other. "Bindy started telling me this strange story about this guy in the bar that wouldn't let her use the phone."

"Did Mom hear?"

"No, she was asleep. Bindy said the guy threatened her. The whole thing really weirded me out."

"So did you ever tell Mom or Dad?"

"No! Bindy made me promise to keep it a secret. Besides, Mom's so stressed with the whale thing, and Dad was all upset about losing Bindy, and I didn't want to give them any more problems, especially if none of it's true. Do you think it's true?"

"I don't know," Jack shrugged. "It all sounds pretty bizarre. Besides, if some guy really did threaten her, why didn't she tell the police? She was in the police station for over an hour, right? It doesn't make any sense she wouldn't tell them."

A wave rolled in, this time licking the toes of their shoes with foam. Neither one of them moved, and Jack felt dampness seep into his shoes. The sea suddenly seemed a deeper gray, colder and unforgiving, as if the sun were hidden behind a cloud. Glancing up, he saw that the sun was shining, just as it had been moments before.

"Bindy said this guy told her he knew where to find her and that he would hurt her. Jack, if he could hurt her, he could hurt Mom or you or me."

Jack pushed his hands deep into his pockets. "I wouldn't worry about it," he said slowly.

"Why not?"

"Bindy makes up stuff. She's talking, that's all."

"How do you know?"

"I know."

"But how?"

"Because I overheard something back home, when Mom and Dad were talking in the kitchen. I'm not supposed to tell."

"Wait a minute! That's not fair!" Ashley blazed. "I told you my secret! What do you know that I don't? Come on, Jack, tell me!"

Jack took a breath, then let it out slowly. His parents had told him not to speak of what he'd overhead, but this situation had changed in a way no one could have guessed. Bindy had graduated to spinning lies that spooked his sister, and that wasn't right. Some things were bigger than rules.

"OK, but don't ever say I told you! It was about why Bindy was put into foster care."

"Why?" Ashley asked, wide-eyed. "I asked, but she never told me."

"Basically, it's because her own family says she's a liar."
"What?"

"I didn't hear what she said her brother did to her, but whatever it was, everyone in the school came to Cole's defense and nobody, not one person—not her aunt or her uncle or anybody—believed Bindy. What does that tell you? Plus, Bindy took that money right off the table at the bar—remember? If she really was going to replace it, she would have put those dollar bills down when she picked up the quarters. I don't believe her. It's like she spins everything, twists every story to make herself look good, but I think it's all just that—stories! I mean, just listen to her talk on and on about all the stuff she says she did. She says she's an actress, but was she really?"

"She had to be!" Ashley protested. "She knew all of Amanda's lines—"

"So what? You've seen that movie so many times you know the lines, too. It doesn't mean anything. The truth is—" Jack hesitated before blurting—"The truth is, Ms. Lopez said it was Bindy's own aunt and uncle, the ones who adopted her, who are trying to get rid of her now because she lies."

"You mean they're the ones who stuck her in foster care? That's awful!"

"Yeah. I know they're not her birth parents, but when you adopt someone, you're supposed to become their real parents, aren't you? Like, be their real mom and dad? Anyway, now they're trying to give her back. How many parents would do that?"

"Jack, *shhhhh!*" Ashley hissed.

No! It couldn't be! In an instant Jack saw a third shadow darkening the sand, and as that realization slammed into his brain, he felt his insides turn upside down. Bindy was behind him! Bindy must have heard everything he and Ashley had been saying! Whipping around, Jack practically ran into Bindy's thick body. A deep flush had crept across her cheeks, and tears glittered at the edges of her lashes, but her eyes were on fire. The chattering Bindy was gone; a smoldering, angry person stood in her place.

"Where—where's my dad?" Jack stammered.

"Back on the path, shooting some pictures of an eagle. I kept wanting to call Aunt Marian, so he let me borrow his cell phone. So, you want proof that I was an actress? *You* call her."

"Uh—I don't—" Jack stammered.

"Go ahead! I know her work number. Call her and ask her if I played Amanda in *Melissa's Dream*. That was the whole reason she took me in. I was a perfect, ready-made, talented little girl to match her perfectly golden son. Only I didn't turn out the way she wanted, did I? Guess that made me disposable. Go on! Hear it from her own mouth. She'll tell you I was in *Melissa's Dream* and on television. I do not lie, Jack! Everything I talked about was true!"

"Then why are they trying to get rid of you ?" Ashley asked softly.

Bindy shook her head, her expression condemning Ashley for her foolishness. "Because my so-called brother Cole used to use me for a punching bag, and I finally tried to stop it. He's smacked me around ever since I moved in with them, and for years I took it and took it—I thought I had to be grateful. Remember, I'm just an orphan!" She spat out the word as if it were poison. "Then one day a speaker came to my school and said, 'The worst secret is the one you hold inside. If someone hurts you, you must tell.' So I told. Look what it got me!" She laughed harshly. "There are things worse than bruises."

"I'm—I'm sorry, Bindy—" Ashley began, but Bindy cut her off. "Forget it. You're just as bad, Ashley. You're just like everyone else. If I were still pretty, you'd believe me. Pretty people don't lie, right? Only ugly ones. The truth is, I don't care anymore what either one of you thinks." Her eyes were gray now, a distant, cold gray that matched the ocean. "Here, let me dial it for you. Ask my aunt. She'll tell you."

Silence suddenly enveloped them, a chill silence as clouds hid the sun. It was as if all the emotion had boiled over into the sea, churning the water and shooting it over the rocks like geysers, and now the very waters reflected Jack's insides. He wished he could take back his words, the same way the waves retreated back into the depths of the ocean. Too late for that. He didn't know how to make it right.

The phone's keyboard glowed orange as Bindy held it out to him, but when Jack shook his head, she slowly let her hand drop to her side.

Suddenly Ashley sprang forward, shielding her eyes. "Jack—Bindy—look at the water!"

"Ashley, we have enough problems here—"

"No, look. I see something. Over there by those big rocks. You see it too, don't you, Bindy? That shape— like a boat—but it's floating upside down or something. It's a dark color."

Bindy rocked onto her toes. "Yeah. I see it."

"Where?" Jack asked, and Bindy pointed the way. Jack squinted until a shape he thought was a rock rolled forward, then was drawn back by the tide. Whatever was out there, it looked at least as big as a rowboat, only thicker.

"Is it a person?" Ashley asked.

"If it is, he must be dead," Bindy answered.

Ashley took a step into the water, and then a second step and a third until she was standing knee-deep in foam. "Jack, I know what it is. Call Dad!" she screamed.

CHAPTER FIVE

"**I**t's a *whale!*" Ashley yelled, splashing into the surf. "I think it's stranding!"

The large, rounded mound rolled closer, but this time it seemed to flounder on the rocks as the waves sucked back to the sea, leaving the animal lodged in shallow water. Its top half was exposed to the fitful sun. If the clouds parted and the sun shone through, its heat could harm the whale in a matter of hours.

The whale didn't move at all on its own but seemed to rock with the rhythm of the sea. For a moment Jack had the sickening feeling it might already be dead. Another wave crashed around it, sending a spray of foam into the air.

"We've got to get Dad—" Jack cried, but Ashley had already plunged through the first swell. Now thigh-deep in seawater, she dashed toward the whale, instinctively slowing down before getting too close. A beat later, Jack plunged in, with Bindy close behind. "Wait, guys, don't rush at him," Ashley ordered when they caught up to her. "You'll only scare him! Move slow."

"Yeah, Bindy, quit splashing."

"I'm *not!* The water—it freaks me out."

Ignoring them both, Ashley gingerly moved forward with Jack right at her heels, while Bindy hovered behind. He'd never seen a whale up close before. The hide was slick and gray, and the grooves below its bow-shaped mouth looked like an accordion-pleated bowl. Fourteen feet long and four feet high, it had beached itself less than ten yards from shore. Another wave swelled around it, rocking its thick body forward like a boat tied to a slip.

"It's OK, we're not going to hurt you," Ashley cooed, inching closer. "We're going to get you back in the ocean, where you belong. Don't be scared. It'll be all right."

"Aren't you guys getting too close? Can't it bite?" Bindy asked.

"I'm not worried about that, but the tail could whip around and hit us," Jack warned. "It would be like getting knocked over by a truck."

When Ashley carefully placed her hand on the whale's back, Jack did the same. The hide felt like wet rubber beneath his fingers. Reacting to their touch, the whale shuddered.

"Look, it's just a baby," Ashley wailed. "Oh my gosh, I can't believe another whale has beached itself! What is going *on?*"

Bindy's voice seemed to thin as she asked, "Is it dead?"

"No," Jack said, pointing. "Look at his eye." He wasn't prepared for how human the whale's eye looked. A sliver of white showed at the bottom lid, and the pupil, liquid and brown, expressed plain, raw fear. This animal was scared to death.

Suddenly it let out a wheezy noise that made Jack jump back in fright. "What was that?" he yelled.

"Sounds like it has asthma," Bindy answered.

"Don't be silly. Whales don't get asthma."

"How would you know?" she asked him.

That was true. Jack knew next to nothing about real whales that stranded themselves, then made little thrashing movements and funny noises like this one did. He was amazed to find, on the top center of the whale's head, not one but *two* blowholes—crescent-shaped slits close together like nostrils.

A large wave swelled forward, pushing with cold force before it curled past to lose its energy at the shoreline. The three of them were suddenly soaked to the middle of their chests. Although Jack could feel the sun on his face, the water itself was frigid. They couldn't stay out here long. His feet were already beginning to go numb.

"Man, I *hate* these waves!" Bindy cried.

"Why don't you go back to the shore and find my dad?" Jack demanded.

"No—I want to help. If we could just push him back into the water....We could grab him by the flippers and pull—"

"No!" Jack caught her as she put her hands against the animal's side. "Not the flippers!" Even though he was a baby, the humpback's armlike pectoral flippers, several feet long, were more delicate than they looked. To pull on them, Jack knew, could really hurt the whale. "Mom said a lot of people try pushing or pulling stranded whales back into the water and just end up hurting them. Anyway, this whale must weigh about two tons. It's too heavy for us to move."

"Well, then, what's your idea? We can't just stand here staring at him! We've got to do *something!*" Bindy declared.

Ashley looked worried. "Mom said that when a whale's out of the water it can't deal with gravity, remember? She said a whale's insides can be crushed by the weight of its own body."

"Yeah, I remember," Jack answered grimly. "Not only that, but the way those clouds look overhead, there might be a storm coming. And if the waves start to whip up real hard, they might dash him against these rocks. That would really be bad."

As if in response, another wave swelled forward, rocking the whale toward Ashley. The bottom three inches of her hair dripped salt water, flattening into ten-drils that looked like black seaweed against her yellow Gore-Tex jacket. Staring out at the ocean, she cried, "Oh my gosh, I think I see another whale! Out there, in the bay, straight ahead. Do you see it?"

Shading his eyes, Jack strained to look. A huge, dark shape moved against the horizon, barely above the waterline, creating a slice that seemed to move against the ocean current. A small puff of water shot into the sky from the blowhole, and then the shape disappeared from view until the scalloped end of its tail flipped into the sky. The mother searching for her baby? Or just a lone whale gliding through the waters? Maybe it, too, had its sonar scrambled by some strange phenomenon. What if it was getting ready to beach itself? The thought spread a chill through Jack, colder than the Atlantic waters. Another animal might wash onto shore. It seemed impossible, yet nothing about these strandings could be considered normal. His sister must have been thinking the same thing, because her mouth grew tight. "Bindy, you've got Dad's cell phone. Call 911."

Bindy visibly paled. "Uh-oh," she gulped.

"What do you mean, 'uh-oh'?"

Jack watched as Bindy reached into her back pocket to retrieve the cell phone. Water trickled out of it in a tiny stream. "I'm sorry. I forgot. I'll get him a new one."

Great! Jack screamed inside his head. Just great! Now they had no way to call. Quickly scanning the beach, Jack looked for any flicker of movement that would let him know someone was there. Other than the gulls, the white sand gleamed empty. Where was his dad?

"Hey, it's not my fault your phone's not waterproof. Maybe it'll still work." Shaking the receiver, Bindy punched the numbers, then held it to her ear. She jiggled it again, then pushed it into her sweatshirt pocket. "Maybe not. I'll go find your dad. Don't worry, we're not that far from the car. He'll find a phone somehow."

"While you're gone, Jack and I will keep the back of the baby whale as wet as we can," Ashley told her. "I remember that's important. I just hope the mamma whale doesn't decide to beach, too. I don't want 40 tons of whale on top of me."

"She's just looking for her baby," Bindy said. "Is that your mamma out there, searching for you? Huh? Oh, you poor little thing." Gingerly, Bindy stretched out her hand, letting it hover over the baby whale as if feeling some energy force emanating from its skin. Then, almost imperceptively, she touched the back of the whale with her fingertips. "I hate to see any animal suffer. They're the only creatures on Earth that don't care if you're fat or thin. Only if you're nice."

"Bindy," Jack began, trying to keep the impatience out of his voice, "you've got to go *now!*"

"But I think I've figured it out. No matter what, I won't let them get away with this," Bindy said softly.

"Look at what they're doing. They're liars who hurt innocent whales. It's not right."

"Who? Bindy, what are you talking about?"

Jack stared at her, and she looked right back at him, her eyebrows arched like two half moons. "What would you say if I told you I think I know why all this is happening?"

Jack held on to his temper. "We don't have time for this—"

"Listen to me! I think the government *is* testing that sonar. I didn't put it together before, when we were in that meeting with your mom—you know, the one with Greg. But I've been thinking about it, rattling the whole thing 'round in my head ever since, until I *have* put it all together. I know, Jack. Our wonderful government is lying through its teeth."

Another one of Bindy's wild stories? Why was she doing this now, when he couldn't possibly have time to pay attention to her ramblings? Jack clenched his teeth so hard he could feel sand grit between his molars. A baby whale was dying, another whale might come sailing on top of them at any second, and Bindy was up to her old headline-grabbing tricks. A government conspiracy? Bindy, possible child star and maybe abused adopted sister, had cracked the case while staying in Acadia less than 24 hours. Right. It was too ridiculous to waste his energy on—he had bigger problems than spies and aliens and all the other bizarre stuff that fermented in Bindy's strange mind. For now, he needed her, though. Keeping his face as smooth as he could, he said, "Make sure you tell my dad about the government thing when you find him."

"Why should I tell him? He won't believe me." Bindy's voice was flat. "No one ever believes me. It's obvious that *you* don't believe me. Even if I know the truth."

From the corner of his eye he saw the whale in the ocean make another pass, closer this time. "Jack," Ashley cried, "that big one's getting near. And we've got to get some water on the back of the baby before it dries out. Start bailing."

"I'm sorry, Bindy." Jack's words came out in a rush as he began splashing at the whale's side. "You'll have to let my dad handle your government conspiracy theory. I've got to keep this guy wet."

"Fine. I'll go now."

Another large wave crashed, but this time Bindy rode it to the shore. She stumbled only once before righting herself to stagger onto the sandy part of the beach. Waddling awkwardly, she made her way toward the steps until she finally disappeared from view. What a wacko, Jack thought.

Ashley started singing an Irish song to the whale, soft and melodic, but Jack could see how stressed the animal was. The whale's eyes rolled back, and every few moments his flukes strained or his tail would thrash helplessly in the surf as he made those wheezy noises.

"*Shhh,*" Ashley cooed softly. "You're going to be all right. But why did you come up here, little one? Don't you know you should never come out of the deep water?"

"Did you hear what Bindy said about the government and the sonar?" Jack asked. "There is something really wrong with that girl."

"Can't worry about that now," Ashley replied. "Feel his skin—it's getting warm and dry on top. You've got to throw water on him. Cup your hands and sling water over his back!"

"Remember to keep the water away from his blowholes," Jack told her. "Mom said they can drown from that."

"Right. We'll start near his tail and work up."

Jack splashed as much as he could onto the baby whale's back, but the tiny scoopfuls seemed as useful as a single raindrop on a garden. There had to be a better way. But what? His shoes? They'd hold little more than his hands did. He began to peel off his jacket, shivering as a wave washed over him.

"What the heck are you doing?" Ashley cried.

"Making a bucket. Here, take two corners of my jacket. We'll scoop the water over him."

Without a word Ashley grabbed the ends and held them taut. Dipping the jacket as deep as they could, they counted to three and pulled up hard. The ends of the jacket ripped out of Ashley's hands and fell into the water, useless.

"I can't—it's too heavy."

"We're scooping too much water. Don't go down so far this time. Wrap the sleeves around your wrists before you pull; it'll give you better leverage."

They dipped his jacket again, this time being careful to go no farther than a foot beneath the waves. "One, two, three!" An arc of water sailed through the air and smacked onto the baby whale's back, trickling down his sides in a smooth sheet of liquid.

"It's working!" Ashley said gleefully. "We got ten times more water on him than we did using our hands. Don't be scared, baby whale, this is going to help you stay well."

"We'll need a system so we can get all of him. Move down one step, and then we'll dip it again. We've got to keep his back wet without hitting the blowholes—we'll need to do his head, but we can do that by hand. Spud needs to stay hydrated until help comes."

"Spud?"

"He's got to have a name, doesn't he? He looks like a Spud to me."

"How long's it been since Bindy left?" Ashley asked.

"I don't know. Ten minutes, I guess. Maybe 15."

Biting the corner of her lip, his sister looked out into the ocean. "The other whale's still out there."

"I know it," Jack replied. "And I hope it stays out there. The big ones almost never survive. It's going to be rough enough for Spud, and he's a baby."

"But we're keeping him wet!"

"You know that's only half the problem. If he's stuck on the rocks when the tide goes out, he'll crush under his own weight. We've got to get him back into the ocean."

"The rescue team will know what to do," Ashley insisted. With a circular motion, she rubbed her hand over the whale. "Spud'll make it."

"I hope they hurry because I'm starting to freeze. This water is so cold! We've got to keep moving." Muscles strained on his back as Jack dipped, hurled, stepped, then dipped again. If it was tough for Ashley, she didn't let on. Every few minutes a wave would knock her off balance, but she'd right herself, take another step, then fling another arc of water onto the whale. When they threw the water, drops flew back onto the two of them, which meant they were both soaked from head to foot.

Time crawled. The waves seemed colder now, turning Jack's feet into blocks of ice and the skin on his bare arms a deep red. He saw but did not feel a strand of kelp wind around his leg. Pulling it free, he flung it away from him like a snake. Where were they? Mentally, he calculated how long it would take Bindy to get to his dad. Ten minutes max for Bindy to get back to the trail. If Steven had gone very far chasing the eagle, it was possible Bindy wouldn't find him easily. Those pine trees were thick, with a tangle of foliage underneath that made walking difficult. No, if she couldn't see him, Bindy would be sure to call out, and Steven would drop everything to come running. The most he should add would be five minutes. That would leave another seven minutes for them to get to the car, followed by another ten to reach a phone. Would he go straight to the Visitor Center, or stop anyone he could find to ask for a cell phone?

Thirty-two minutes there and at least as many back. With a sinking feeling, Jack realized this wouldn't be over any time soon. Another thought, unbidden, crept into the corners of his mind. *If* Bindy even went for help. What if she just took off and left them all? She was acting so strange, nothing seemed impossible. The color of Ashley's lips was deepening at the edges, as if she'd sucked a blue Popsicle, and he could see her teeth chattering. She had to get out of the water.

"Go to the shore and get warm, Ashley. Then I'll go, and we'll switch places."

"N-n-no. It takes both of us to get water on S-Spud."

"He won't dry out that fast. Listen to me, you're turning blue. You can't help Spud if you freeze to death."

"I'm OK."

"I'm telling you to do it!"

"But—"

"Ash-ley! Ja-ack," a faint voice cried. "We're coming."

Even from a distance Jack could recognize his mother's voice. Soon his father and a group of five rangers swarmed onto the beach like ants, some carrying coolers while others had blankets and buckets.

"They're here!" Jack yelled. "They got to the beach pretty darn quick."

Relief flooded Ashley's face. "I knew Bindy would pull through."

"Yeah," Jack agreed. "I've got to admit I wasn't sure. She was acting so weird, I didn't know what she'd do."

The two of them barely got to shore before they were shrouded with blankets that felt as warm as toast to Jack. His mother hugged him tight for just a moment, whispering how proud she was into his ear before reaching over to give Ashley a squeeze and saying, "You guys stay here and warm up. I've got to see about saving that baby humpback."

"Sp-Spud," Ashley chattered. "J-Jack named him."

"I'm sure Spud is very grateful. The humpbacks are endangered. We need every single one of them."

"Where's Dad?" Jack asked.

"He and Bindy followed me in his car. I couldn't believe it—the two of them burst into my meeting at the Visitor Center, and then the rangers jumped up and got gear while I called Allied Whale to tell them to send their rescue team. Then we raced down here. The rescue team should be here any minute."

"There's another whale out there, Mom," Jack told her. "I'm afraid it might beach, too."

Olivia peered into the ocean, then shook her head in disbelief. "What is going on? Not once before this has there been an incident of a whale beaching in

Acadia National Park. This is nothing short of disaster. I just don't understand any of it!"

She was zipping herself into a wet suit when the eight-member Whale Rescue Team arrived. In minutes every one of them had put on wet suits, too—blue or red or black. Each person on the beach seemed intent on only one mission now, to save the baby humpback.

Special blankets for keeping his back wet were dipped in water and applied to Spud's hide. Olivia quietly waded in with a long needle to take a blood sample, which would be analyzed at the local hospital. Someone smeared zinc oxide on Spud's blowholes to keep them from drying out, while two other team members used a suction cup to fasten a platelike device onto the baby whale's back.

"That's a TDR—a time-depth recorder," Olivia explained. "When we get Spud back into the ocean, that will let us know whether or not he's swimming out to where he's supposed to be. It'll fall off after a couple of days."

"How are you going to get him back into the ocean?" Jack asked.

"Look over there." Steven, who'd been taking pictures nonstop, pointed to a man and a woman. The two rescue-team members were carrying a huge harness toward Spud. By the time they dropped it onto the rocks next to him, the tide had begun to come in a bit stronger. Jack could hear the rescue-team workers talking about what they planned: As soon as the tide-waters became deep enough, the eight of them would work together to refloat Spud, gently wrapping the harness around his pecs and tail to guide him back to the water. It wouldn't be easy.

Even though Jack felt cold and wet, one sight he didn't want to miss was Spud being returned to the ocean where the mamma whale waited for him. He felt excited for Steven, too, because photographing this whale rescue would be the chance of a lifetime for his father. His photos might be printed in *USA Today,* or even—and this was Steven's dream—in *National Geographic!*

As Jack wrapped the blanket tighter around himself, he noticed Ashley shivering. "Pretend you're not cold," he whispered to her. "I don't want Mom or Dad to send us up to the Visitor Center, because then we wouldn't get to see everything. Anyway, I'm not that cold." And that was true. He'd felt the blood return to his feet and then his hands. At first the tingles hurt, but soon they subsided, and he felt as if he could last for as long as the rescue took—hours, if necessary.

"I'm cold, but I can stand it. What about Bindy, though?" Ashley asked. "You know how she complains about everything."

Jack turned all the way around, searching as far as he could see across the crescent of Sand Beach. "I don't see Bindy. Where is she, Dad?"

"She should be around here somewhere. She said she'd be driving down from the Visitor Center with your mother."

"Well, I can't see her."

At that moment, Olivia waded out of the surf, looking pleased by the progress being made by the rescue team. "Mom, where's Bindy?" Ashley asked.

"Your father brought her," Olivia answered.

"No I didn't. She told me she was going to ride with you," Steven said. "You mean she wasn't with—"

"No!"

"Then where—"

Jack dropped the blanket and looked wildly around the beach. Every single person milling about was a park ranger or wore a jacket marked "Allied Whale Rescue Team."

Bindy was gone. Again.

CHAPTER SIX

"I'm sorry, Dad," was all Jack could think to say.

"It's not your fault. It's mine." The sun streamed into the interior of the car, shadowing the deep frown lines between Steven's eyebrows. "I should never have believed Bindy when she told me she was going with your mother," he said. "I should have put her in the back seat of the car myself and buckled her in with my own hands. Or I should have made sure Olivia knew I was leaving Bindy with her. She told me she wanted to watch the rescue squad save the whale, but, then again, Bindy is not to be trusted. Obviously." He slammed the heel of his palm into the steering wheel. "Now I'll have to go back to the police and tell them she got away from us again. This time they might take her away from us for good."

"Not if we find her first," Ashley said.

"I hope we do, kids. I surely hope we do."

The scratchy gray blanket the rangers had given Jack rubbed damply against the backs of his legs. The park rangers had said both he and Ashley could return the blankets tomorrow, which was a relief, since standing on the shoreline had chilled him thoroughly, and their car was parked a distance away. Sniffing, he realized they'd have to wash his blanket before returning it. It smelled dank, like seaweed mixed with salt. He licked his lips, tasting salt on them, too.

Ashley, who had her blanket wrapped around her papoose style, leaned as far forward as her seat belt would allow to announce, "I think Bindy's gone after the conspiracy people."

They'd already told Steven the story about the government cover-up, which he didn't believe any more than Jack did. "That's just too ridiculous to even consider," he said now. "Bindy just made up another tall tale to impress you."

"Then where do you think she went?" Jack asked.

"My guess? She's probably trying to get back to her aunt. Maybe she thinks running away from us will prove to her family how much she wants to stay with them. Who knows what goes on in that girl's mind?"

"I don't even care why she ran away," Ashley fumed. "It's just plain selfish—she never thinks about anyone but herself. Now you can't take pictures of Spud, Dad, all because of her."

Steven drew a sharp breath. "And I'll have to contact Ms. Lopez. Boy, I'm not looking forward to making that call. How do I explain to her that I lost the girl—twice? Ms. Lopez will have to let Bindy's family know, of course. This could get ugly."

For as long as Jack could remember, his father had lectured him about obeying the posted speed limit, but this time Steven was pushing it a lot faster than he should. Oak trees and pines streaked by in a silver-green blur. Jack could feel centrifugal force pressing him against the side of the door as Steven sailed around a bend. Ashley shot Jack a worried look; Jack shrugged in reply.

"Dad," Ashley cried, "slow down."

When Steven hit the brakes, Jack snapped forward. "Kids, I want you both to look for Bindy while I drive," he said. "It's a long shot, but it's possible she decided for some strange reason to walk back to our motel. Although she doesn't have a key to the room. But then again, the lady at the front desk would probably let her in if she asked."

"We're watching for her, Dad," Jack assured him. "Ashley's taking the left side, and I'm looking out the right. If she's out there on the road, we'll spot her."

Not that checking the roadside would do much good. Bindy would never have made it this far, at least not under her own steam. A few cars passed by as visitors entered the park, but not many cars were leaving. Jack saw a biker in an apple green helmet whizzing along on razor-thin tires, plus one woman on a motorcycle, then another trickle of cars and a Hummer. But no Bindy. She'd just vanished.

Pressing his forehead against the glass, Jack watched the spruce and oak trees fly by. Acadia was breathtaking. The whole park seemed to have been gilded with yellow-gold, not the autumn kind that meant the approach of winter, but the bright sun gold of early summer. Boulders appeared every now and then, like large stone turtles, and every so often the trees would part to reveal a slice of coastline. The ocean looked more gentle from a distance, with tiny whitecaps that laced the ocean like bits of frosting, but Jack wasn't fooled by its benign appearance. His skin was still cold from standing in the 50-degree waves that had chilled him to the bone. Tightening the blanket underneath his chin, he pictured a hot shower, dreaming of how amazingly good it would feel to steam himself half raw. That was the first thing he'd do. The second thing would be to wash out his running shoes, since they were beginning to smell like fish.

"Kids, I know you're cold and wet, but could you bear with me while I take a quick check of the town? The chances are pretty slim that we'll spot Bindy on the streets, but I'd like to give it one last shot before I have to—" His voice turned grim. "To go to the police."

"No problem, Dad," Jack and Ashley both agreed.

Moments later, Steven turned down a road that led him to the main street of Bar Harbor, their first chance to see the town in daylight. Brick storefronts were shaded by scalloped awnings, wedged between small wooden buildings that had been painted the colors of gourmet jelly beans.

"Wow, this town is so cool! When can we come back for a real visit?" Ashley asked.

"I have no idea," Steven told her. "This trip has turned into a nightmare. You'd better take it all in now."

Knots of tourists milled along the sidewalks, peering into windows or walking hand in hand, some with peppermint-striped paper bags from the candy shop, others carrying shopping bags filled to overflowing. Wooden signs with all kinds of pictures decked the shops: One had a blue fish, another a lobster, and a third showed a family of bears carved into wood. There was no sign of Bindy, and no way, Jack decided, they could find her by driving aimlessly. Steven must have figured it out, too; without a word, he headed for the Seaside Motel. After he dropped them off, he'd go to the police.

"You have your key, Ashley?" Steven asked as they pulled into the parking lot.

She held it up. "I've got it."

"Good. Would you please run up to the room and check and see if by some wild chance Bindy is there?"

"Sure, Dad." Ashley unbuckled her seat belt, saying, "Be right back."

Since the steps leading to the upstairs rooms were outside the building, Jack could see his sister quickly scramble up and run to her door, which was only three down from where the steps ended. A moment later she disappeared into the room.

Steven sighed and pushed a lock of blond hair off his face. He seemed in no hurry to move, and Jack didn't want to rush him, so he sat perfectly still and waited. Glancing at his father's profile, Jack noticed that Steven looked different than he had just a few days before. His jawline had softened, and there were pouches under his eyes that seemed smudged with gray. Bindy was wearing him out.

Ashley appeared at the door and shrugged her shoulders, hands spread apart, palms up.

"Well, as I suspected, she's not there," Steven said, his voice tense. "All right, Jack, you're in charge. I want you two to *stay put* in the room until I get back. If Bindy shows up or phones the room or you hear from her in any way, I want you to immediately call your mother's cell phone. Mine's still with Bindy. It's not working, of course. Seawater will do that. I tried to dial the number countless times, just in case it started working again and she'd perhaps answer, but...nothing." Raising his sunglasses, he rubbed the bridge of his nose. "Remember, I'll be checking with your mother every 15 minutes to pick up messages."

"We'll call if we see or hear anything. Promise."

"Good." He gave a quick wave as Jack scrambled out of the car, and then, tires squealing, he drove away.

Ashley was already using the shower in the connecting room when Jack arrived. He turned on his own shower, standing in the hot steam until his skin turned the color of the lobster he'd seen on the Bar Harbor sign. Lathering up his hair, he rinsed, then lathered again, letting the bubbles run down him in foaming sheets. He could think in here.

The Landons had lost Bindy twice, which meant his family could be in legal trouble—being a foster parent involved a lot of responsibility. The Bar Harbor police already had a record of Bindy escaping once, which could be bad. Two times might make them think of negligence. What if Marian, Bindy's adoptive mother, decided to sue them? Even if she herself didn't want Bindy, she might be the type to cause trouble if she thought the Landons hadn't done their job properly.

Jack stuck his head under the water to wash away the thought. He was most likely borrowing trouble. No one would go after his parents, not when they were trying so hard to help. His dad had been a foster child himself, shuttled from one family to another before living his teen years on a ranch for boys. Over and over again, Steven had told Jack to reach out to those who weren't as fortunate.

"The easiest thing in the world is to slip-slide into an attitude of entitlement, especially living in this country," his father had told him. "I want you to see real heroes—kids who've been knocked around by life, yet still rise up to take on the world. I want you to see what it is to have grit. Your mother and I want to make a difference in the lives of unfortunate kids." Now it was Bindy who was making a difference in the Landons' lives. Except it wasn't for the better.

When he came out of the bathroom, he found Ashley spread-eagled on one of the beds, her wet hair spiraling onto the comforter.

"Took you long enough. I was out ten minutes ago, and I'm a girl."

"I didn't know we were racing."

"Doesn't matter," she said, grinning. "I still won."

"Yeah, right."

"Jack?"

Jack sat on the other bed, looking at his sister. "What?"

"I have an idea, but I don't know if it's an OK thing to do. Remember how I went through Lucky's stuff in Mesa Verde and everybody yelled at me for doing it? You said her things were private, and I was totally wrong for going through them."

Jack nodded. He remembered. Lucky was one foster child he would *always* remember.

Winding a lock of hair around her finger, Ashley asked, "I was wondering if this time, with Bindy, I mean, if this time is different enough to check out her things. We might be able to figure out where she's gone. It's just, Mom and Dad are totally freaking out, and—"

"I think it's a great idea," Jack jumped in, mad that he hadn't thought of it first. "You look in her dresser drawer, and I'll see if there's anything in her suitcase."

Ashley bounded off the bed, hurrying into the room she'd shared with Bindy, while Jack went to the corner where the suitcases were stacked. Bindy's battered blue one was at the very bottom of the pile. Pulling it free, he snapped open the locks and opened it. Nothing. Even the pockets were empty.

"Jack, come here!" Ashley cried. "Wait'll you see this!"

Rushing through the connecting door, Jack saw Ashley standing in the middle of the room, holding up a crumpled towel and rolled-up clothes. Bindy's clothes.

"These were in the bottom drawer. She was here, Jack."

"How? When?" Jack stammered.

"I don't know. But I'm positive this is the outfit she had on when we were with Spud. The clothes are wet, and they smell like seawater. So she got back here to the room somehow to change." She held up the towel, as wilted as a lettuce leaf. "Looks like she showered, too. I didn't see any of it before because I didn't look in her drawer. What a little sneak!"

"Is the rest of her stuff still here? Her other clothes? Toothbrush?"

Nodding vigorously, she said, "Yep, all of it—well, I don't actually know about her toothbrush." She went to their bathroom and pushed open the door. "Her toothbrush's here, and her earrings, too. I don't get it— if she was actually running away, wouldn't she have packed up her stuff?"

"You'd think so," Jack agreed.

"We need to call Mom."

Jack crossed the room to the square table that held the phone. Once he had an outside line, he punched in the numbers and waited. After three rings, a message kicked in:

You have reached Dr. Olivia Landon at the Elk Refuge in Jackson Hole. If this is an emergency, please call the Jackson Hole Veterinary Hospital. Or, if you'd like to leave a message, please....

"She must be on the phone," Jack mouthed to Ashley. When he heard the beep, he said, "Mom, it's me. Bindy was here, at the motel. We found her wet clothes and a towel stuffed into a drawer. Call me when you get this."

He dropped the receiver into the cradle, then sat on the edge of Ashley's bed. So, Bindy had been here. What on Earth was she up to? If she'd been running away, it stood to reason she would have wanted her things—it would have taken only minutes to pack. Was she trying to fool them, keep them all off balance? Or was there something worse going on?

Ashley looked as confused as Jack felt. Sliding into one of the green corner chairs, she stared out the glass door that led to their balcony. Her fist rested on her cheek so that Jack could not see her face. "I don't get it," she mumbled, more to herself than to Jack. "I just don't get it."

Jack called his mom again, and got another recording. After trying again he said, "I'm going to go out on the balcony. Maybe the air will help me think."

He opened the sliding glass door that led to the balcony, with its Astro-Turf carpeting and white plastic chairs. A four-foot-high metal railing, once painted white but speckled with rust, caged him in. Beneath him was a rolling lawn, green and trimmed, and then the rocky shoreline that led to the water's edge. To the left stood the long pier with its chain at midpoint.

Leaning on the railing, he studied the long pier. That's where he'd been last night, at the end of it, where the weird stranger had wanted to know his name. Because of the darkness, Jack had never gotten a good look at the stranger, but in daylight, the pier looked innocent. The same small rowboat, tied to the pier near the shore, still bobbed gently in the water. Gulls wheeled through the air while a band of ducks waddled out from a cluster of trees.

Jack's thoughts needed sorting out. What did he really know about Bindy? No one at her school believed she was telling the truth about her brother Cole beating her up, again and again. Her adoptive parents didn't like her—that much had come from Ms. Lopez. But did that actually prove anything? An idea nibbled at the edges of his mind. What if she'd been telling the truth? What if the problem was that Marian and her husband didn't want to take Bindy's word—Bindy, the adopted girl who'd turned out to be such a disappointment—against the word of their own flesh-and-blood son. What was it Bindy had said? Jack searched his memory. *Only ugly people lie; that's what everyone thinks.* Bindy wasn't ugly, but Jack could tell she believed she was.

The phone rang, causing Jack to jump. Finally! Ashley was still sitting in the chair as he hurried inside.

"It must be Mom," he told her as he reached for the receiver. "She must have gotten my message." Placing the receiver to his ear, he said, "Hello?"

"Hi, Jack. Surprise, surprise." Although there was a lot of static, the voice on the other end of the line was unmistakable.

"Bindy?"

"It's me."

"Where the heck are you?" Jack shouted. "Do you have any idea how worried—"

"Just quit talking, Jack. I baptized your dad's phone in the Atlantic, remember? Even though it dried out, it's still not working too well. I don't know how long it will hold out."

"Where are you?" he asked again, softer this time. Ashley had run over to where he stood, watching him with wide eyes.

"I like that red shirt you have on now. You should wear red a lot—the color looks better on you than that yellow jacket you wore this morning."

"What?"

"I saw you on the balcony, Jack. Like, two minutes ago."

"Where are you? Why did you run?"

"Because you wouldn't believe me. No one ever believes me. But now I have proof. So listen carefully. I want you to walk toward the pier, but not all the way. Stay to the left. You and Ashley go to that jagged place in the rocks, the one covered with all the barnacles and stuff. Do you know which place I mean?"

"Yes."

"And then I want you to walk around the shoreline. There's no one over here. Meet me in ten minutes."

"We're not allowed to leave!" Jack protested.

"Ten minutes," Bindy told him.

The line went dead.

CHAPTER SEVEN

"Sh-she's out there," Jack stammered. "Bindy—she said she wants us to meet her on the shore. Right now!" Ashley's dark eyebrows shot halfway up her forehead, and her voice came out even higher. "You know we're not allowed to leave this room. We can't go."

"I tried to tell her, but she didn't listen. She said she could see me standing on the balcony, which really creeps me out. She said we had ten minutes to meet her, and then she hung up."

Ashley didn't wait for Jack to finish. Banging open the sliding door, she ran to the balcony and waved wildly, calling, "Bindy! Bin-dy!" When she leaned over the railing so far that her head seemed to disappear, Jack grabbed her by her belt loops, yanked her back, and set her down with a thud. "She can't hear you. She's way too far away." He pointed to the rocky coast where she'd told them to meet her, slicked wet with ocean water and kelp. The tree line began just beyond the rocks—tall, cone-shaped pines, dark and full of shadow, that seemed to guard the land from the sea. Was she hiding in there, watching both of them now?

"We've got to call Mom and tell her what's happened," Jack said grimly.

"Bindy said ten minutes. How much is left?"

Jack glanced at his watch. "Eight minutes."

Hurrying back inside, he grabbed the phone and punched his mother's cell number. Come on, Mom, be there. Answer this time. Come on!

You have reached Dr. Olivia Landon at the Elk Refuge in Jackson Hole. If this is an emergency, please call the Jackson Hole Veterinary Hospital. Or, if you'd like to leave a message, please....

Slamming the receiver into its cradle, he yelled, "I don't believe it! Who the heck is she talking to?"

"The park people are probably using it."

"Yeah. Maybe you're right."

"Should we call the police?"

"Bindy will be gone before they can get here."

He began to pace the room, stopping at the sliding glass doors, looping back to the bathroom, then back to the balcony. Ashley sat on a bed, cross-legged, her dark eyes following him. For a second time he called his mother, this time leaving a message. After a third attempt, he found himself fidgeting at the motel door; he could feel Ashley staring at him.

"You're not seriously thinking of going out there."

"Got to," he snapped. "Time's past up. If I could ever get through to Mom, she'd probably tell us to go after Bindy. I've got to find her and make her come back."

"Why?" Ashley thundered. "Just let her go. She's nothing but trouble."

Jack's voice was just as hot. "You don't get it, do you? Just think about how bad it could be for Mom and Dad if Bindy disappears. They're the ones responsible for her! It could get really, *really* ugly, and I'm not going to let that happen."

With her thin arms crossed tightly over her chest, Ashley said through tight lips, "What if Dad comes back and finds us gone? It could get *really, really* ugly for you and me. I don't want to get grounded for the rest of my life because of that—troublemaker!"

But Jack wasn't listening. He'd been over all of it in his mind, and there was no other way. He had to at least talk to Bindy, convince her to come back. If that failed he could try to force her, but the truth was, Bindy was a year older than Jack and 40 pounds heavier. The thought of trying to wrestle her into submission was ludicrous.

Yanking on his wet shoes, he gave instructions to Ashley about what to say when she finally got through to their mother, but when he looked up, Ashley was already pulling a navy blue sweatshirt over her head. "I'm going, so don't even start," she announced. When he hesitated, she said, "It's my family, too, Jack. I'll write a note for Dad and tell him what's happened."

"Well, write it fast. We gotta go."

Bits of seashell crunched underfoot at they made their way to the cove, and his shoes still squished from their dunking in the Atlantic. The rocks had some sort of sea plant growing all over them, slimy and thick and brown; it looked like the whiskers on a walrus's face. It was easy to slip here, and it stank. Flies swarmed at him, vanished, only to reappear moments later, buzzing his ears like mosquitoes.

"Man, these flies are nasty," he told his sister.

"I think they're hanging around those tide pools in the rocks—there's a lot of dead stuff floating in them. Let's get up where the trees are. It'll be better there." Ashley, who had always been nimble, scrambled over the rocks as easily as a cat. It wasn't so easy for Jack. With his arms outstretched like airplane wings, he tried to keep his balance but slipped at every turn.

Bindy was nowhere to be seen. He knew there was no use calling out to her. If she'd watched them clamber up the rocks, she would know exactly where they were. No, in her own good time, Bindy would come to them. Ashley had already settled onto a rotting log. He joined her, scooting to the side when he discovered he'd sat squarely on a knot.

"How long now since she called?" Ashley asked.

"Twenty-eight minutes."

"She said we had to get here in ten. Do you think she left?"

"Maybe. But I don't think so." Straining for any human sound, Jack looked overhead into the thick criss-cross pattern of spruce branches. Wind rustled the pines, causing them to shiver in the perpetual dusk of their shade. Sounds were muffled by a thick layer of needles that carpeted the ground. Where was Bindy?

"So you came," was the way she greeted them.

Jack whirled around to see Bindy standing five feet behind him, making her usual dramatic entrance, leaning against a tree with one hand high on the trunk and the other on her hip. She wore a pair of faded jeans and a blue-and-green plaid flannel shirt that hung past her hips in loose folds. Her hair fell in damp strings. If she was worried about running away, she didn't show it.

"Yeah, we're here," Jack nodded. "And what about you? How'd you get back to the motel? You couldn't have walked."

"I hitched," she answered. "This sweet old lady stopped to give me a ride. I told her that my car had broken down a ways back, and I needed to get to the motel where I was staying."

"Your car! Like you were driving your own car?" Jack scoffed.

"You think I can't play the part of a 16-year-old? Watch me."

Right before their eyes, Bindy seemed to grow older. She straightened up, flipped back her hair, pulled in her cheeks and looked—16.

"OK," Jack said, "but now you have to come back with us to the room. Bindy, do you have any idea how much trouble you've caused? My dad's driving all over Bar Harbor, frantic! He thinks you've run away. He's gone to the police, and he'll have to call Social Services in Wyoming to report that you're gone. Do you know what that means? You could get taken away from us."

"Not that you'd care. Now maybe someone will listen to me. That'd be a first!" Bindy laughed harshly.

Ashley rolled to her feet, facing Bindy squarely, demanding, "Are you coming back with us or not?"

"What about what I found out? Don't you care about that?" When neither Jack nor Ashley answered, she said, "I know why the whales and all the other marine animals are dying. I can prove it."

"Come on, Bindy," Jack answered scornfully. "Is this that government conspiracy thing? That was pretty lame—"

"Shut up and listen to me!" she blazed. "I heard a man talking in the bar." She closed her eyes as if trying to remember—or maybe she was just rehearsing. When she opened them, she began, "I was waiting for the pay phone. At first I wasn't really listening to what he was saying because I had other things on my mind—like what I was going to tell Aunt Marian. Should I say that even though I told about Cole beating on me, I wasn't actually trying to get him into trouble, wasn't trying to make him lose his scholarship or anything? Cole has this big football scholarship to Duke University, did I tell you that?" She didn't wait for any acknowledgment, but went on so fast it seemed one word touched the next. "Or, should I tell her I know they love him more than me, but now I'm OK with that? He's their own son, right? Anyone would love their own child more than their adopted niece. Don't you think?" Bindy's question was tinged with sadness; how was Jack supposed to answer it? He remained silent.

"So all that was going through my head. Then I started to get impatient, because this man kept talking to Alex, whoever he was. He kept saying, 'You better have the money, Alex. These techie guys want to get paid right away. They're yammering that sonar components are pricey to build and the suppliers need to be paid off. The price is up 'cause it's a rush job.' I didn't know what 'sonar components' meant, and right then I didn't care. But the man said it a couple more times—sonar components—and then he goes, 'I got the parts right here at my feet.'"

Now Bindy appeared more intense, leaning forward as though she really wanted to convince them. "I looked over to see what he was talking about, and there was this square metal case, like a suitcase, only silvery. He said, 'I'll wait at the pier till midnight.' Whatever this Alex answered got him upset, because he said, 'I thought you were the one in the big rush. If you don't show by midnight, I'm gonna leave it with the bartender. You can get it from him tomorrow. Yeah, the bartender's my partner. He'll be counting the cash, so don't try any games. God bless America.'"

"God bless America?" Jack questioned.

"Don't interrupt. So all of a sudden he saw me, and he slammed down the phone. He said, 'How long you been sitting there?' and I told him, 'Not long.' He stared at me with the coldest eyes, and he asked me, 'You know what I'm doing here?' I shook my head no, because really, I had no idea what was going on, and I didn't care— I just wanted to use the phone. But then, after about a minute, he goes, 'What I just did on the phone is my business. Anyone who messes with my business messes with me. I don't think you'd want to do that. If a person repeated my phone conversation—to anybody—I'd consider that messing with me. People who mess with me end up dead.'"

"Oh, come on, Bindy," Jack scoffed. She had to be making that up.

Confused, Ashley looked at Jack, and asked, "What does any of this have to do with the whales?"

"*Sonar components!*" Bindy cried. "Weren't you listening? That ranger said the government had sonar that could blast out a mammal's ears, but the government wasn't using it. Right? Well this guy was obviously selling sonar to the Navy—he even said God bless America."

"Why does it have to be people in our government?" Jack asked.

"Because they're the only ones buying. Who else would even want sonar? That has to be the answer!"

"Bindy, you're totally guessing. You don't know if anything you heard has anything to do with the sonar that blows out the mammals' ears," Jack protested. "You don't have any proof."

"I know it in *here!*" She pushed her finger into her gut.

"Here," Jack said, pointing to his own stomach, "isn't worth much. The whole thing makes no sense. If the Navy needed sonar components, why would it be getting them from some sleazebag who left them in a bar in Bar Harbor?"

"Conspiracy, conspiracy, conspiracy!" Bindy practically danced as she hissed out the words. "Think about the facts. Fact: A whole bunch of animals are washing up onto Acadia's shore. Fact: That's never happened before. Fact: Sonar blew out the eardrums of the whales in the Bahamas. Fact: The animals in Acadia have the same broken eardrums. Face it—everyone says they're not sure what's causing it, but we know it has to be the sonar. We can *prove* it." She jerked her fingers through her hair, pushing her locks apart in damp rows. "We have to."

If Jack hadn't known it before, he knew it now. She really was crazy. Bindy, with her mousy hair and thick, plain features, had somehow blurred the line between television and reality. It was as if she thought they were in some spy show, with bad guys and techno-gadgets and a possible happy ending all wrapped up into a tightly-written script. But this wasn't television, this was reality, and the only thing he cared about was getting her back to the room. Let his parents deal with Bindy's lunacy. He just wanted out of the middle of it all.

A couple of gulls flapped through the air to land beyond the swells, feet first, onto the slate gray water. They began to squabble and bicker loudly before settling down, bobbing on the waves. That's what Jack wanted to do. He'd like to float for a while, instead of struggling to keep his family's head above water. For a moment he was half tempted to walk away from it all. Then he thought of his parents.

"Bindy, my folks'll get in big, massive trouble if you leave. Will you please come back with us?" Even Jack could hear how weary the question sounded.

"Yes."

The answer took Jack by surprise.

"I'm so glad," Ashley breathed. "I mean, I thought you were going to—I'm just so glad you'll go with us. Dad's been so worried, driving all over, trying to find you. This is great. Mom and Dad can maybe investigate that sonar thing for you." Ashley stood, brushing flakes of bark from her jeans.

"Wait—not so fast." Bindy held up her hand. "I'll come back to your folks and be a good, obedient foster child, but on one condition."

"A condition?" Jack frowned. "What condition?"

"You have to come with me first. I have a plan. See, I watched your face when I told you my story, and it was the same old thing. You didn't believe a word I said."

"That's not true," Jack lied, embarrassed that he'd been so transparent.

"It's just like with Cole. No one will believe that my gorgeous adoptive brother would slap me around, not even when I showed them the bruises. But now you guys have got a problem because your folks are on the hook with me takin' off like I did. So here's the way it'll be." Leaning an elbow on her thrust-out hip, she wagged a finger at them and said, "You help me, and I'll help you. With this deal, there are *no* negotiations."

Ashley looked at her quizzically. "Where do you want us to go?"

"Back to the bar." Bindy grinned defiantly. "We're going to steal us a silver box."

"*What!*" Jack couldn't believe he'd heard her right.

"Actually, not me, Jack-o. You! I can't go bopping back into that bar—the bartender knows me. It's gotta be you. Unless Ashley—"

"You leave my sister out of this," Jack stormed.

"Well then—" Bindy tossed her head at him as she declared, "It's you, you, you. Say yes, or I take off this minute."

Talk about being between a rock and a hard place! He was standing on a slab of shore rock that suddenly felt as big as the whole state of Maine, while this lunatic demanded that he sneak into a bar and steal some imaginary silver suitcase. If he didn't humor her, his parents would get in a whole heap of trouble. If he *did,* he might get hit over the head with a baseball bat. In movies, bartenders always seemed to keep baseball bats behind their bars.

"OK," he said, giving in. "Tell me what you want me to do.

"Jack!" Ashley protested. "You're not going to go along with this—"

"Yeah. I am. Me and me alone," he answered. "You stay out of it. Go back to the room and—"

"Forget it!" Ashley had that look on her face again, the stubborn look that meant Jack might as well save his breath, because Ashley would do what she wanted. He groaned. Now, on top of everything else, he had to worry about keeping his sister safe.

"Here's what'll happen first," Bindy was saying. "We'll put together the whole scene like a movie script— dialogue, action, and me as the director." As she began to outline her plot, Jack felt his stomach sink to his toes. This was a role he definitely did not want to play!

CHAPTER EIGHT

Smokey's Bar looked like the kind of place for hard drinks and harder people. Situated less than half a mile down the shore from the Seaside Motel, Smokey's sat squat in a cluster of trees 50 feet from the shore, a plain rectangle with a flat roof and tin chimney. The building was made of wooden logs stained tobacco brown, with one small shuttered window that reminded Jack of a patched eye. The only decoration of any kind was a neon sign that read "Beer and Spirits," which Jack could hear humming faintly in the distance, like mosquitoes at dusk. This was not like the other buildings that dotted the shoreline. Smokey's looked rough.

"Go around to the back, where no one can see us," Bindy hissed. "Keep your heads down, but don't act weird, like you're trying to hide something. Just be natural."

"We *are*," Ashley retorted.

"I'm just telling you that as an actress, I've learned how to get into character."

Ashley rolled her eyes at Jack, who shook his head back. There was nothing either one of them could do. Bindy had them caught in her web, and the only strategy Jack had left was to get it over with as fast as he could. Feet crunched on gravel as the three of them made their way through the back parking lot, stopping behind a garbage bin to make sure no one had seen them. He did not want to go into a bar. He did not want to steal a metal suitcase. He did not want to get caught and face the same officer that had arrested Bindy. The whole plan was nothing short of insane.

"OK, do you remember what you're supposed to do?" Bindy whispered for the 70th time.

"Yes. Create a diversion—"

"—and make sure you believe what you're telling them, or they'll see right through you and know you're lying," Bindy interrupted. "Make your story good. Act. Once you start this, you can't back out."

"You do realize I'll be stealing," Jack reminded her.

"No you're not. You'll be preventing a crime. Fight fire with fire, that's what I say."

He tried again. "If I get caught, I go to jail."

"Then remember two points," Bindy said, holding up her fist. "Number one"—her index finger punched the air—"it's not really stealing if, by taking the object, you stop a much bigger crime, like the killing of the whales. Number two—" She held up her middle finger and grinned, "Don't get caught."

"Gee, thanks for the great advice."

"What if we get the suitcase out, and there's nothing in it?" Ashley demanded. "Then what?"

"Then we sneak the case back to Smokey's, and I go home with you. Case closed. Agreed?"

Jack nodded, while Ashley stood frowning, with her lips pursed.

"Once you get inside, Jack, you'll see the bar on your left and the pay phone straight back at the far end of the wall. It's still pretty early, so there won't be that many people in there."

"That's good, isn't it?" Jack asked.

"Yes and no. The downside is you'll really stand out. That means you need to go straight to the bar to do your thing. You ready?"

Jack wasn't, but he nodded again.

"All right. It's show time!"

Taking a deep breath, Jack squared his shoulders. He could do this. Think of his parents and how much they needed this, he told himself. And don't get caught. For sure, don't get caught.

Since it was only five o'clock, the parking lot stood almost empty except for an old van and a rusted BMW. Acting as if he belonged there, he crunched up the gravel path, pulled open the door and stepped inside. The bar was dim and hazy, as if Smokey's had settled for a kind of twilight. It took a moment for Jack's eyes to adjust. He blinked, trying to pull the scene into focus. The tables sat empty except for a couple of men hunched in a small booth in the back. The wooden floorboards had pathways worn where the veneer had been scuffed away. A bartender had been wiping down the counter with a towel, but when Jack approached he stopped in mid-wipe. He stared at Jack coldly.

"Hi," Jack said, giving a halfhearted wave.

"Hey, kid, you can't come in here," the bartender growled, "unless you're 21. You don't look 21. Unless you're some kind of a dwarf. That what you are? A dwarf?" He laughed at his own joke and said, "I already got in trouble with a kid in here, and I don't need no repeat performance. Beat it." He was an older man with a face grizzled by sun and salt. Thick gray eyebrows cast deep shadows over hooded eyes. "You deaf?" he demanded, rubbing the countertop once again.

When Jack didn't answer, he barked, "I said get outta here, kid. You're in the wrong place."

"There's...there's...." Jack could hardly get the words past the lump in his throat. His parents, Sunday school, the Boy Scouts—every institution he believed in taught that his word was his bond. Now he was going to lie outright. Well, once Bindy kept her promise, he told himself, he could sort out the rest. For now he had no choice.

"There's water shooting out of the back of your building," Jack told him.

The bartender's eyes grew wide. "*Where* out back?"

"I don't know. I was walking by and I saw it and I thought you might have broken a pipe or something. I thought you should know."

"All I need is a stinking plumber bill...." The bartender smacked the towel down on the counter and ran along the hallway toward the back exit, leaving the bar unattended.

Jack tensed. This was it! No one was watching him. Feeling a thousand pricks of adrenaline, he hurried behind the bar and looked underneath the counter. At first all he saw were cabinets and row upon row of liquor bottles, tall and short, fat and thin, with all kinds of foil labels in brilliant colors. Then—a flash of silver! So, at least that much of Bindy's story was true. Looking around one last time, Jack saw no one. As quickly as that, he grabbed the suitcase and began to sprint to the door. It was heavy! His knees almost buckled beneath him.

"...don't see no water," the bartender's voice shot back. "So what is this, a trick?" Jack could hear the anger rising in his voice. "You some kind of prankster? Hey, kid—what are you—" His voice turned deadly. "*Give me that case!*"

Jack ignored him. Yanking open the door, he bolted out into the parking lot and raced toward the trees where he was to meet Bindy and Ashley.

"*Drop it, kid,*" the bartender bellowed. "*Now!*"

His heartbeats hammered in his ears as Jack dove into the trees. Where were Bindy and Ashley? For a crazy moment, he thought Bindy might have set him up, but then he saw them hovering behind a knotted pine.

"Go! *Go!*" Jack shouted. He couldn't waste breath explaining anything—carrying the heavy case took a lot of energy, and they all needed to run. Tree limbs snapped at his face as he took the lead into the woods, the leaves churning beneath his feet like dust. He could hear Ashley and Bindy crashing behind him—or was that the bartender giving chase? Did the bartender have a gun? The thought, which he hadn't considered before, scared Jack. Would he get shot for stealing a suitcase? Curling his back as he ran, he thrust forward like a runner breaking through a finish line. He could almost feel the bullet in his spine.

"Jack! Wait!" Ashley cried.

Jack whirled around, and when he did, the suitcase banged against a tree with a thud. "I better not break whatever's in there," he muttered. "Not after all this."

"Jack, I said wait! It's Bindy—we're losing her." Ashley had stayed right at Jack's heels, but Bindy trailed behind. Scanning the woods, pushing panic down, Jack forced himself to wait. A moment later he saw Bindy's round figure struggling up the hill, but nothing else. The bartender seemed to have vanished.

When Bindy finally caught up to them, she bent over, hands on her knees, breathing hard. She panted,

"Good work, Jack-o. You got the case. And we lost that old dude. He'll never find us now."

"Are you sure he's not still back there?" Jack asked.

"Might be. But I kept turning around—he gave up a long time ago. He won't find us now."

"Don't be too sure. We need to get back to our room and stay there."

"What about the case?" Ashley asked.

Jack tightened his fingers around the handle. "What about it?"

"Should we open it to see what's inside?"

"Not here."

"Why not? Let me see it," Bindy demanded.

Jack clutched the heavy suitcase to his chest. "No. We don't open it. Not until we're in our room."

Bindy's eyes narrowed. "What are you saying, Jack?"

"I'm making sure you keep a bargain. I did my part, now you have to keep your end of the deal."

"So you still don't believe me."

Jack didn't answer.

"OK, fine," Bindy said, sweeping out her arm. "Lead the way."

They kept to the trees, winding their way toward the Seaside Motel. They could tell they were heading south by watching for glimpses of the bay. Jack didn't want to get too far afield, and yet he still wasn't sure the bartender wasn't back there, lurking among the trees. Finally he saw the roof of their motel, slate-colored and flat. He could feel himself relax. They were almost there. One road, then a parking lot, then the steps, and they would be home free.

"Just walk natural," Bindy instructed. "Act like you own the road. No one will notice you if you act like you belong."

She was right. No one seemed to pay the slightest bit of attention to the three of them as they sauntered across the road. By the time they hit the parking lot, Jack could almost taste the safety of his room. Up the stairs the three of them clambered, not even bothering to be quiet. When he finally opened the door to his room, Jack collapsed on his bed and threw the suitcase down beside him.

"We made it!" Ashley cried, dancing around the room on her toes. "We got Bindy back. We need to call Mom and tell her! I hope she can find Dad. Whew!"

"So open the case," Bindy urged. "You'll see that I was right. It's some kind of sonar thing to kill whales. I'm not making it up. Open it."

Jack heaved himself to his feet to stand over the case. Ashley and Bindy hovered behind him. It was an expensive piece, like nothing he'd ever seen before. Brushed to a satin finish, it reflected his face in a warped blur, his blond head featureless, distorted. It reflected Bindy, too, who stood so close he could feel her breath on his neck. He inched away from her.

"Come on! Do it!" Bindy cried.

He hooked his thumbs on the tabs on either side. "Well, here goes." He pushed on the tabs. Nothing happened. Hooking his thumbs harder, he tried again.

Ashley frowned. "What's wrong?"

"I don't know. I think it's locked."

"Locked?" Pushing Jack aside with her hip, Bindy yanked the tabs so hard her face reddened. "Uh," she said, slamming her fist into the top. "I don't believe it— the jerk locked it. We need to get the key! Maybe it's under the counter. Maybe it's in the cash register."

Despite the warm, stale air in the room, Jack felt a cold chill spread through him. "You're not serious."

Bindy shoved her fists into her pockets and stared at Jack. She nodded decisively.

"We are *not* going back, no way. Look, I've already stolen for you. I'll be giving this thing back to that bartender guy, but that doesn't change the fact that I took it in the first place. That's trouble enough. Now you're talking about a stupid *key?*"

"But Jack, how can I prove—"

"Forget about that. I did what you asked, it didn't work, and that's the end of it. I'm through breaking the law. And if you really want us to believe you, you'll keep your word and stay here and wait for my mom and dad. You promised."

Bindy stood with her head bowed. Silence filled every corner of the room as Jack held his breath and waited. Different scenarios seemed to flash across her face, one after the other as she weighed her options, her fists still jammed into her jeans so that the pockets bulged, her brows knit tightly together. It was Ashley who seemed to know what to do. Gently, as if she were coaxing one of her baby animals, Ashley guided Bindy toward the glass double doors, saying, "Why don't you get some fresh air? Just sit out there and watch the waves and think. I need to let my folks know you're back. They're going to be really happy about it."

Without a word, Bindy sank into one of the plastic chairs on the deck. On the ground beneath the deck, ducks waddled happily, quacking loudly at nothing, but Bindy didn't seem interested. She kept her eyes focused on her shoes. Jack couldn't help noticing she looked utterly defeated.

When Ashley stepped back into the room, she put her finger to her lips, signaling to Jack to be quiet. "I'm going to close these curtains a bit. Jack, we need to talk."

They crossed to the bathroom, the farthest point from the balcony, so they could talk without Bindy overhearing. Ashley's dark, anxious eyes searched Jack's face. "I'm worried we can't keep her here," she whispered. "I'm not so sure she'll stay. Then we'll be right back where we started."

"At least we're better off than we were two hours ago," Jack told her.

"Except we have to get the suitcase back to the bar. I still can't believe you had the nerve to steal it."

"I couldn't think of any other way to help Mom and Dad. I'll just have to take it back and explain and hope that bartender doesn't kill me. If that works out, then I think we'll all be home free."

"Yeah," Ashley smiled. "Home free."

Suddenly a fist pounded against the door so loudly it made Jack's teeth chatter. "This is the police," a deep voice boomed. "Open up!"

CHAPTER NINE

"The *police?*" Ashley cried.

"I already know you stole from Smokey's Bar," the voice barked. "My name is Officer Norton, and I'm with the Bar Harbor Police Force." Pounding again, he said, "Don't make it any harder on yourself. Open the door! I've got my badge right here—look through the peephole, and you'll see it."

Jack felt his insides turn to ice. So the police already knew. Now he couldn't go to the bartender and beg for mercy and smooth it all over—no, thanks to Bindy, it was too late for that. He'd been caught stealing, something he'd never done before, something he'd never do again. What would his parents say? He stood there, numb, as Officer Norton banged again. "Kid, I know you're in there! Give me that suitcase!"

"I don't see any badge," Ashley said, peering out.

Pound, pound, pound.

"Jack, we can't just stand here," Ashley told him.

Pound, pound, pound!

Officer Norton's voice became deeper, more insistent. "If you cooperate, I might forget the whole thing. Smokey just wants his case back." There was a pause, and then, "Did you hear me? *Open the door!*"

"Should I let him in?"

"I don't know!" Jack cried. "I don't know what to do!" His mind had gone blank. Hide the case and deny it all? Get it back to the bar on his own? Call his parents? Or just confess and take his punishment? Ashley moved to the door and waited, her hand hovering over the doorknob.

"You're only making it worse! Open up!" Officer Norton demanded.

"Jack, we've got to let him in. He's a policeman." Opening the door a crack, Ashley peered outside. Suddenly thrust backward, she let out a cry as the door almost knocked her off her feet. The man had pushed himself inside. His eyes quickly scanned the room.

"That's a smart girl," he told her, slamming the door shut. It made a sickening thud behind him. "So there's two of you. Anyone else?"

He looked nothing like the police officers Jack had seen. Tall and thickly muscled, with a large, bulbous nose, he stood with legs planted far apart. Greasy hair had been slicked back, and he smelled of cigarettes and diesel fuel. He wore no uniform, just a long black coat that skimmed the top of heavy boots. Just like—just like—the man on the pier! Jack was almost sure of it! This was no detective, it was the man from last night! And they'd let him waltz right in. Jack's palms got wet with sweat.

"I asked you kids a question. Is anyone else here?"

"My parents. They'll be back in a minute," Jack lied. "They just went down to get a newspaper."

Ashley glanced at him sharply, then looked away. Wrapping her arms around her chest, she held herself so tightly her shoulders seemed to swallow her neck.

"That so?" the man answered coolly. He opened the bathroom door and peered inside. "There's a newspaper in here. How many newspapers do your folks need?"

Jack didn't answer.

"Don't try to play me, kid. I get real angry when someone jerks me around. And you don't want me to be angry, do you?"

Jack tried to keep his face smooth as he asked, "Why aren't you wearing a uniform?"

"I'm working undercover."

"Could I see your badge?"

The man reached inside his coat and pulled out a leather wallet. He flipped it open quickly, but when Jack moved closer, he snapped it shut and slipped it back inside his pocket.

"We didn't get a chance to look—" Ashley began.

The man ignored her. "Where's the case?"

She pointed. "Right there, Officer Norton."

"Go get it for me."

Grunting at the weight, Ashley snatched up the case and handed it to the man. He tried to open it, realized the tabs were still locked, and grinned. "So, you didn't mess with it. That's good. Smokey'll be real happy to hear you weren't diddling with his stuff."

"We didn't touch it," Ashley assured him. "Are you going to arrest us?"

"Now that depends. Smokey's a friend of mine. I was just two blocks from his bar when he calls me all panicked. He says some blond kid told him there was a flood out back of his place—busted pipe or something. Told me the boy walked right in and lied to him, then ran off with his case. That was you, wasn't it, Jack?"

"How'd you know my brother's name?" Ashley asked.

"Oh, I'm a very good detective."

Jack wondered how long the man would keep up the officer myth. Ashley still seemed to believe it. Well, it might be better that way. Don't challenge him, and maybe he'll take the case and leave, Jack hoped. Right now, that was the only goal in his mind. Get this man out of their room.

"See, I'm smart," the man said, tapping his temple. "I remember all kinds of things. Like, for instance, last night. I met young Jack on the pier. He told me he was staying right here, in this motel. I remember that. And

I remember telling him to mind his own business. Too bad you don't listen, huh, Jack?"

He pulled out a knife, a long switchblade, and flipped it open. Calmly, he began to run the tip beneath his fingernail as if he were cleaning it. Jack felt hairs rise on the back of his neck.

"But what I don't understand is why you took the case in the first place. It troubles me. How'd you know about Smokey's? How'd you know anything?" He leaned against the door, blocking it with his heavy body, and continued to flick the knife's tip around his nails. "So, why'd you take it, Jack?"

"I don't know."

He shook his thick head. "See, I think you're lying again. I warned you not to do that. Looking at Ashley, he asked, "What's your name?"

"Ashley. I'm his sister."

"Ashley, I think you need to tell brother Jack here that he's got some explaining to do. There's booze under Smokey's bar. And money in the cash register. But your brother Jack goes right for the silver suitcase. Can you tell me why?"

"I—I...."

"Give me a reason, Ashley, and I won't arrest either one of you. Tell me why he wanted the suitcase. That's all I need—a simple explanation."

"Ashley—*don't!*" Jack cried, but it was too late. His sister's words were already tumbling out of her mouth.

"We thought the silver case had some sonar stuff in it—there are whales dying and we thought some Navy guy named Alex was using sonar and we were trying to get the sonar so we could prove that the whales were being killed—"

"*Alex?*"

"I think that was his name. Anyway, we didn't know if it was true, but we thought we could check and then put the case back—"

"How did you hear about Alex?" The man's eyes suddenly grew charged with fury. "Tell me!" he thundered. "How did you know? It was that fat girl, wasn't it? The one in Smokey's last night. She must have been the one you were looking for on the pier, right, Jack? Where is she?"

"Gone," Jack lied. Taking a deep breath, he tried to remember all the instructions Bindy had given him about acting. *Look confident. Make eye contact—don't let your glance shift away from the person's face.* "She never came back last night," he said, staring at the man. "She's a foster child, and she ran away before I saw you on the pier. We never found her. We looked all over the place, and then my parents reported to the police that the girl was gone."

"Jack...."

"Ashley—*shut up!*"

Ashley stared at Jack, ready to say something. Then, all at once, she got it. This was no policeman standing in front of them!

"Does anyone else know about this? *Does anyone else know about Alex?*" he shouted.

"No one. She only told me," Jack said, not wanting to reveal Bindy's name, if the man didn't remember it from the night before. "She told me right before she ran away. I—I might have mentioned a little bit to Ashley, but she doesn't understand anything. She just heard the words, but they don't mean anything to her. I swear!" He was shaking inside, but he prayed it didn't show, prayed that the man would believe him. Jack, who'd hardly ever lied in his life, was making up for it now— big time! "You said if we gave you an explanation, you would let us go. We told you what happened. We're supposed to meet our parents by the front desk. They went to buy a newspaper."

The man laughed at this. "Well, now, Jack, looks like you and me have a lot more in common than you thought." His eyes widened so that Jack could see tiny red veins, and when he leaned close, Jack could smell stale cigarettes on his breath. "You're lying about where your parents are, and—guess what! I lied, too."

With a motion as fast as a snake, he caught Ashley, pulled her back against his chest and jerked her upward, the blade within an inch of her throat. Ashley recoiled as she tried to pull her neck away from the knife point. For one nauseating second Jack realized how small his sister was. Her legs dangled above the floor like a rag doll's.

"Jack, I want you to listen carefully. When we walk out that door, we will be one big happy family. Understand? We will all take a stroll to the pier. Then the three of us are going on a boat ride."

"Boat ride?" Jack asked hoarsely.

"Yeah. You messed up the pick-up arrangements, so now I have to deliver it myself, and you two are going with me. If you try anything, Jack, anything at all...." He pulled the knife away from Ashley's neck and set her back onto the floor. "I'm not a violent man, not unless someone makes me that way. Don't make me hurt your little sister." He touched her cheek with the blade of the knife, the other hand still clamped onto her shoulder. "I'd hate to have to teach you a lesson, Jack. But I would. Remember that. Now pick up the suitcase." He waved the knife toward the door. "You go first. My little girl Ashley will be right by me—" Suddenly, he froze. "What was that?"

Jack heard it too. A scraping noise came from the balcony. Bindy! He'd half forgotten she was out there! Had she listened in? Did she know what was happening? Jack's heart felt as if it would explode right out of his chest as the man zeroed in on the glass door. The curtains, which were half shut, hid most of the view. There was no place to hide out there. Jack could feel himself stiffen as he pictured the man finding Bindy.

"Are you still playing games with me, Jack? Is someone out there?"

"No!"

"Well, now, this will be your first test. Let's see how well you do. If you are lying, your sister pays the price." He narrowed his eyes at Jack. "Don't move a muscle." Clamping Ashley around the neck, the man dragged her toward the balcony, yanking open the glass door with the hand that held the knife. As the man's head swiveled from side to side, Jack held his breath until the blood pounded furiously in his ears, as loud as drums. He waited for Bindy to be discovered, but a moment later, the man pulled his head back inside.

"There's a bunch of ducks out there, that's all you heard," Ashley babbled. "No one's out there. Let me go! You're hurting me."

"Shut up and move," was all the man said.

Bindy had escaped! The scene flashed through Jack's mind like a neon sign—Bindy must have climbed over the balcony into the adjoining room, the one she shared with Ashley. She would call for help, and the police would catch up to them before they had to enter the boat! Call, Bindy, call! Jack willed her. Hurry!

Herded through the door, along the front deck and down the motel stairs, he tried to buy time by pretending that the heavy suitcase slowed him down even more than it did. The man had tucked Ashley beneath his left arm, his overcoat practically swallowing her like a blanket. His right hand, still clutching the knife, was hidden in his pocket. Anyone watching would have thought it all looked perfectly normal. A father, daughter, and son enjoying one last view of the ocean before they checked out of the motel. Jack looked around, desperate to see anyone who might help. He heard wheels clacking along a walkway, and moments later saw a mother pushing a blue stroller, her child's round head bobbing as the woman maneuvered around a corner, disappearing without a glance in their direction.

"Go to the pier," the man ordered. "If anyone looks your way, just smile and nod. Smile and nod."

They followed a narrow path strewn with crushed shells and gravel all the way to the water's edge. An elderly couple returning to the motel strolled past them on the path, close enough to touch, but they were deep in conversation and didn't look their way even once. The rest of the beach was empty except for the gulls. A steel gray wave curled, then crashed onto the beach, licking the sand with foam before slipping back to the sea. It smelled like fish and damp wood here. Jack strained to listen for the sound of a siren but heard nothing save the screeching gulls. They were utterly alone.

"Now climb onto the pier. You remember the pier, don't you Jack? It holds a special memory for me."

Without a word of protest, Jack stumbled along the boards, followed by Ashley and the man. Shadows from the railing made a pattern on the bleached wood pier, black on gray. "Move it!" the man said, shoving Jack in the middle of his back.

The pier seemed different in late afternoon light. At its end, he saw the wooden steps—gallows steps, he thought now—and something else that hadn't been there the night before. Tied to a wooden piling, a speedboat bobbed like a seagull in the black water, only inches from the landing.

The man hurried them down the rickety steps, gestured to the boat, and ordered Jack, "Put the suitcase in there first. Then you get in."

Where were the police? Surely Bindy had called them by now! Jack didn't want to climb into the boat, but when he hesitated, the man moved his arm under his overcoat, and Ashley cried out in pain.

"I'm getting in," Jack cried. "Leave my sister alone."

"Do exactly what you're told. We're going for a ride."

Jack felt helpless—totally and completely helpless. No one could see them from where they were, no boats were in the marina, no people sauntered along the beach, no police had come to save them. There was nothing to do but obey orders. Stepping into the boat, he felt it rock beneath him. The man maneuvered himself on board with Ashley still clamped to his side. When a wave swelled, the boat thrust up and then down again.

"Sit," the man ordered Jack. "There." He pointed to a seat with a red cushion. Jack sat, his spine as straight as if it had been lined with steel. He looked around but saw nothing he could use as a weapon.

"Put your hand on that rail. Do it!"

The metal of the boat's railing felt cold against Jack's wrist as he laid his hand on it. From a pocket the man took handcuffs that he snapped first onto Jack's wrist, then onto the railing, tethering Jack to the boat. The vessel itself was his anchor now, and there was no way out. If it sinks, he thought, I'll drown.

Moments later, as the motor roared to life, Ashley sprawled onto the floor, sliding on her stomach toward the back of the boat. The man had secured the suitcase so it wouldn't slide, but he didn't care about Ashley.

As they sped into the waves, wind churned against them, making Jack's eyes blur with tears. He could make out Ashley crawling toward him on all fours, her hair whipping into a black cloud, her shirt puffed out like a sail. The motel shrank in the distance to the size of a child's toy, then to a dime, then to a single piece of confetti. The wake sprayed into his face, chilling him. Turning in a wide arc, the boat headed for the open sea, and the man, shielded by glass, lit a cigarette. Jack felt hate surge through him as he frantically pulled against the handcuff. The metal bit into his skin.

Ashley rocked to her knees, grabbed Jack's waist, caught her balance, then placed her mouth as close as she could to Jack's ear. "What are we going to do?" she cried. Her eyes looked terrified.

"You need to—"

"What?"

The noise was deafening. There was no way the

man could hear them over the motor's roar. Louder this time, Jack yelled, "Take this cushion and jump overboard. It'll float." The words seemed to fly back into his throat as the wind beat against him.

"No—no way. Anyway, he'd just come after me."

They were moving so fast the nose of the boat rose above the water until it pointed to the sky. Ashley held on to Jack with a viselike grip. "I'm so scared."

"Me too. But there's—" Even with the noise of the motor and the wind, he didn't want to say the name out loud, so me mouthed "Bindy." "She'll call the police. She heard. She knows!"

"Jack—they might not believe her!"

The thought chilled him more than the spray from the wake, slamming into him like a fist. It was true. Bindy had told so many fantastic tales in the past! He knew how unbelievable the story would sound to his parents, to the police, to anyone who would listen as Bindy tried to convince them: *The three of us stole a case full of secret sonar equipment, part of the government conspiracy that hurt the whales, and a strange man in black kidnapped Jack and Ashley and made them get into a boat.*

It sounded utterly preposterous. Just another one of Bindy's lies added to the pile.

Jack closed his eyes, and in the darkness behind his lids, thought of what lay ahead. Their only hope rested on Bindy.

CHAPTER TEN

Wind cut against Jack, salt stung his cheeks, and the roar of the motor nearly deafened him. When would this ride be over? Still kneeling, Ashley clung to him, burying her face against his arm. Whenever the boat lurched, tossed by a wave, she hung on him even tighter. His left wrist, handcuffed to the rail, grew numb; his right arm, clutched by Ashley, began to ache. How much longer? And where were they being taken?

Jack squinted at the sky. In Maine in the month of May the sun didn't set until around 8:00, he had noticed the night before. Jack tried to read his watch, but the face of it was so covered with moisture from ocean spray that he couldn't make out the digital numbers. The sun was behind him, which meant they were heading east. He couldn't turn around to get a look at the sun's position because the handcuff, as well as Ashley's clinging, trapped him into a cramped position. Taking a guess, he figured it must be somewhere around six in the evening now, a full hour since the man—whose name Jack still didn't know—had come bursting into their room.

The roar of the motor suddenly changed pitch, dropping lower as the boat began to slow down. A thousand feet ahead of them, a much bigger boat sat at anchor—they were heading straight toward it! The pilothouse on the top deck had been painted white, but a dull red covered the walls of the cabin on the lower deck. Attached to that deck was a huge spool wound with cable, probably used to raise and lower the anchor, or maybe it had something to do with sonar.

As they got closer, Jack estimated that the boat had to be about a hundred feet long. It dwarfed the speedboat they were riding in. When they pulled alongside, the man secured the boat then jerked Ashley roughly by the arm and forced her to climb ten feet up a rope-and-wood ladder to the boat deck. Next, he hurried back down to grab the suitcase, leaving Jack behind, still handcuffed to the railing.

Scared, Jack wondered how long he was going to be left there, a captive in the speedboat. After what seemed a long time but was probably only a few minutes, the man returned for Jack. "Now you," he said, after unlocking the handcuff. "Get up there with your sister."

Jack quickly climbed the ladder because the man was right behind him, prodding him hard on the back. When he reached the deck, he found Ashley shivering there, all alone, looking cold and small and fragile.

Suddenly a voice assaulted them over a loudspeaker. "Scully, what the crud have you done? Where'd you get these kids? What are they doing here?"

Scully! So that was the name of the man who'd kidnapped them! Scully looked up toward the pilothouse and called back, "I'll explain everything when you get down here, Alex."

In seconds a door burst open above them. Descending as nimbly as a monkey, Alex clattered down a ladder and dropped to the deck, saying, "OK, Scully, start talking." Thin, wearing black pants, a short black jacket, and a black stocking cap, Alex had a high voice for a man almost six feet tall. "Explain this to me, and it better be good if you expect to get the rest of your money." In a gesture of angry frustration, off came the black stocking cap, revealing spiked blond hair and a smooth pale forehead. Jack noticed long, thick lashes and—he couldn't believe his eyes! Alex was a woman! A pretty woman, who looked younger than his mother!

"Did you bring the device?" she demanded.

"It's over there." Scully pointed to the suitcase. "About the kids, it's a long story, Alex. To make it short, they found out about the sonar."

"How! How could they possibly find out?"

"Like I said, it's a long story."

"You!" She strode toward Scully, her finger pointing accusingly. "You screwed up big, and your timing stinks. I don't know what we're going to do with these kids because Hashim's on board, demanding to witness one more test."

"Where is he?"

"In the galley with the crew, eating supper, but he'll be up here soon. Give me the key to the suitcase."

Scully mumbled, "I don't have it."

"*What!* Oh, for crud—" Crouching down so that her feet stayed flat on the deck while her long legs bent completely in half, Alex yanked a screwdriver from her pocket and forced open the suitcase. "We need to do a test as soon as I install this, because a chopper will pick up Hashim in a couple of hours. We gotta prove to him that this new sonar will work in the shallow waters of the Persian Gulf."

Jack kept his face perfectly still, trying not to react to the words "Hashim" and "Persian Gulf." He was smart enough to know that learning names and places could be dangerous. How many times had he heard on TV, "If I tell you that, I'll have to kill you!" And there he stood, getting an earful of what surely must be secret information.

Ashley had no such concerns—she spoke right up. "You're not going to test that sonar again! You've already killed too many whales with it. You promised you wouldn't do it again."

Surprised, Alex asked, "Who promised?"

"You! The U.S. Navy!"

Scully guffawed, while Alex shot him a dirty look.

"Ashley," Jack muttered, "these people aren't part of the U.S. Navy."

Still scowling, Alex said, "Well, I was once. I worked on sonar technology."

"Yeah, until she got kicked out," Scully said, still grinning. "Dishonorably discharged for conduct unbecoming an officer and a gentleman."

"Gentleman!" Alex spat. "That's what's wrong with—hey, I don't have time to deal with garbage right now, so just shut up, Scully!" She turned her attention to the suitcase, lifting the lid.

At last Jack got to see what was inside. At first all he noticed was thick Styrofoam, layered to hold tight whatever the object was so it wouldn't shift around. Alex tore off the Styrofoam and threw it on the deck. Then, bending forward, she lifted—a plate?

It looked like a plate, but as she picked it up Jack saw that it was a heavy steel rim painted yellow, with bolts all around the edge and in the center, a sheet of thin, shiny, crinkled black metal. The whole thing measured about 18 inches in diameter. What it might be was impossible to guess.

"It ticks me off that those geeks charged me a

quarter of a million to rebuild this part after the exper-imental one broke," Alex was complaining. "That's as much as I paid for my whole boat."

Scully answered, "Yeah, but this boat is an old tug from back when they shoveled coal into the boilers in the engine room."

"Right, and why'd I buy an old tug? Guess! Because it doesn't arouse suspicion. A year ago, this 'old tug' was fitted with an 800-horsepower diesel engine, get the picture? And now it'll have a phenomenal sonar sys-tem, once I ditch the defective part and install this state-of-the-art acoustics transducer. Nobody else will have anything this good for the next five years. Any-way, I gotta go tell Hashim the part's here," she said, hoisting it. "So what do you plan to do with these two kids, Scully?"

"Throw them overboard."

Ashley gasped and Jack jerked backward, ready to run, but where could he run to? It was like being on a tiny island, with no escape.

"You're joking, right?" Alex asked Scully.

Coldly, he answered, "I'm not gonna screw up a ten-million-dollar operation because of a couple of nosy brats. You got any better ideas?"

"Me?" she cried. "Hey man, they're your problem, not mine. But let me tell you, I'd prefer not to have any kids murdered on my boat." Alex spoke calmly, as though she were discussing a maintenance problem.

"So whatever you do with them, I don't wanna know about it."

What did that mean? If Scully murdered Jack and Ashley on the boat, it would be OK as long as Alex didn't find out?

Trust Ashley to always spout off at the wrong time. "I guess if you're the kind of person who murders whales, Alex, you won't worry about killing *us*. But, listen, if you let us go, I promise we won't tell anything." She held up her right hand as though taking an oath in court.

"Like I believe that," Alex scoffed. "I can't waste any more time on this, Scully. Do whatever you have to." Cradling the sonar device in her arms as if it were a baby, Alex turned her back on them and walked through the cabin door.

Jack and Scully eyed each other. Ten feet of deck separated them, enough to give Jack and Ashley a slight head start if they ran. Jack had no intention of standing still and letting Scully kill them—not without a fight. They'd run first, and maybe find someplace to hide.

As Scully reached for his knife, Jack yelled, "Go", as he shoved Ashley away from him; whatever direction she ran, he'd move the opposite way, hoping Scully would chase him and not Ashley.

She sprinted toward a ladder that reached from the deck they were on to an upper deck behind the pilothouse. Jack hesitated for a split second until he was sure Scully was focusing on him, then ran toward the giant spool wound with inch-thick cable, scrambling behind it and crouching down. He heard Scully's heavy boots slamming on the deck, then a few seconds of silence while Scully tried to see where Jack had gone. Those seconds would give Ashley time to locate a hiding place on the upper deck, he hoped.

When Scully spotted him, Jack leaped to the top of the huge spool, grabbed the base of the flagpole, and hoisted himself onto the upper deck. He couldn't see Ashley, but that was good. It meant she'd found shelter.

Swearing, because he was too big and heavy to swing himself up the way Jack had done, Scully ran back around the deck to the ladder and started to climb. Looking around, Jack saw two freestanding structures, one of them a shed about the size of his bedroom closet, and the other one was—a smokestack! Left over from when this old boat burned coal in its engine room.

He heard her then, a soft call, "Jack! Up here."

It was Ashley, *inside the smokestack*, clutching the edge of it, white-knuckled, with both hands. Ashley, always nimble, had somehow scaled the smokestack, even though its top stood a good ten feet above the deck. How did she do it? Jack realized she must have climbed to the top of the shed and from there jumped over to the smokestack, slithering inside it.

Scully's swearing sounded closer, so Jack thought he'd better try the same escape. Looking for toeholds in the rough wood, he dug in with the rubber tips of his sneakers and made it onto the shed's roof, but not before Scully saw him. Knowing that Scully, who was already panting, couldn't climb up there very fast, if at all, Jack stood poised to jump—but not to the smoke-stack. That would show Scully where Ashley was hiding. Instead, if Scully started to climb, Jack would jump straight down on him, hoping to knock the big man onto the deck and kick the knife out of his hand.

"Jack, look!" Ashley screamed. That was when Jack heard it—the thump of rotor blades on a helicopter. Alex had said a chopper would be coming to pick up Hashim—that must be it. Jack wondered where it was going to land, since it looked too big for the deck. It was about half as long as the whole hull of the boat.

And then he spotted the most beautiful words he'd ever seen: "U.S. Coast Guard."

Painted bright red, with a broad white stripe near the tail, the helicopter hovered over Jack like an angel. He stood up and raised his arms, waving wildly. Beneath him, he saw Scully running, probably to warn Alex. In the distance, two Coast Guard vessels skimmed the waves, moving fast toward the boat.

While the chopper hung overhead, wind from its rotor nearly blew Jack off the roof of the shed. Then, amazingly, the door of the chopper opened and a man wearing a helmet and a harness was lowered on a hoist. Toward Jack!

"Get my sister!" Jack yelled as loudly as he could to be heard above the roar of the rotors. He gestured to the smokestack where Ashley was hiding, her head now poking out like a jack-in-the-box. The man gave Jack a thumbs-up, then maneuvered the hoist toward Ashley. After he reached down to grab her around the waist, he slipped a rescue sling over her head and under her arms, then signaled someone in the helicopter to raise the hoist. With her rescuer hanging beside her on the hoist, they were safely inside the chopper in less than a minute.

The helmeted man, still on the hoist, pointed to Jack and then pointed to one of the Coast Guard vessels that had almost reached the tug. So Jack was going to be picked up by boat! As thrilled as he felt over the arrival of rescuers, he also felt a pang of disappointment. Ashley got lifted on a hoist into a helicopter, while Jack would be rescued by boat. It wasn't fair.

Suddenly an amplified voice boomed at Jack, "Wanna do it her way?"

Jack nodded furiously. Immediately the hoist snaked down toward him, with the helmeted man soon dangling above Jack's head. Thrusting his arms quickly through the rescue sling, Jack felt the hoist move upward, and then he was flying! Instead of pulling him up into the chopper, the pilot moved slowly over the nearest Coast Guard vessel. Gently, as though Jack were a spider on a strand of silk, the chopper lowered him to the deck, where waiting arms caught him.

CHAPTER ELEVEN

"It looks just like a white castle," Ashley exclaimed.

"No, it looks like a lighthouse," Bindy corrected her. "'Cause that's what it is—Bass Harbor Head Lighthouse. It was built in 1858, and, according to this brochure, it stands 56 feet above the mean high water mark."

When Ashley murmured, "Well, it looks like a castle to me," Bindy put an arm around her and teased, "You're such a romantic. Maybe *you* should take up acting!"

"No way! I'd rather save whales."

Steven's voice floated up to them, "Kids, come down the stairway—you've got to see the ocean from here,"

As Ashley and Bindy followed the path toward the stairs, Jack called after them, "Tell Mom and Dad I'll be right behind you guys. First I want to get a few shots up here." He'd brought his camera to Acadia, but with all the exciting things that had happened, he'd hardly had a chance to take pictures until now.

He checked his camera settings as he moved around to get the best view of the lighthouse. Ashley was right, Jack decided—Bass Harbor Lighthouse did look like a miniature castle, rising from a cliff that overlooked the ocean's endless blue-green water. A small roof of red tile capped the big lights at the top of the tower. Once the sky darkened, those lights would come alive, sending out beams like *Star Wars* light sabers. Jack could imagine himself inside the lighthouse, scanning the ocean for tall, masted ships; it would be like living in a postcard. He kept clicking the camera's shutter until he ran out of film.

After their exploration of the lighthouse, they drove to the nearby town of Bass Harbor and found a small restaurant huddled in a row of brightly painted stores. Inside, Jack and Ashley sat opposite their parents while Bindy perched on a chair at the end of the table. Since this was Bindy's celebration party, she'd been allowed to order anything she wanted from the menu.

She set down her spoon and stared ruefully at half of a chocolate fudge nut sundae still in her dish. "Whew, that's enough!" she exclaimed. "Even *I* have a limit. But I hate to waste it."

"It's all right, Bindy, you can waste it," Jack told her. "After all, it's your third one."

To stifle a giggle, Ashley covered her mouth with

her hand, getting a bit of chocolate on the tip of her nose. That made Bindy giggle, too.

"Wasting a fudge sundae isn't important," Olivia commented. "Wasting a life—that's tragic."

"You're thinking about Alex?" Steven asked.

"Yes, former Lieutenant Commander Alex Turner, the technical wizard with no moral principles. Greed got in the way of that brilliant mind. What a waste!"

"And she's so pretty, too," Ashley said. "She could have been anything she wanted to be. A model!" When Bindy glared, Ashley stammered, "Not that good looks mean anything! Anyway, Bindy, you said everyone believes you if you're beautiful. Well, no one believes Alex now. She's in jail. Maybe forever."

"For selling technology secrets to the enemy," Bindy agreed.

"And that punk Scully is in jail too," Jack added vehemently. "I hope he stays there till he rots."

"Take it easy," Steven told him. "They'll both get what they deserve."

Olivia reached over to wipe the chocolate off Ashley's nose just as Ashley asked, "Dad, I still don't understand everything about how you found us. Tell me one more time."

Steven answered, "Luckily, I got back to the room within minutes after you two were abducted. Bindy had been trying to call the police, but they weren't paying any attention to her, and neither would I, at first, and

I feel really bad about that now. Anyway, she dragged me out onto the balcony to show me where the boat had gone." Steven paused. "It just happened that I already had my strongest telescopic lens on my camera, so I was able to see the boat and take pictures of the direction it was headed. After that, everything fell into place."

"That's the part I want to know about. Keep going, Dad," Jack urged.

"It all worked out because of our nation's homeland security program—that, and our incredible communications system. I talked to the Bar Harbor police; they called the Navy. The Navy was keeping an active file on Alex, so they knew about the boat she'd bought." As he spoke, Steven traced circular patterns and lines on a paper napkin with his fork, explaining, "They plugged into a surveillance satellite that within minutes located the tug in the Atlantic. It even spotted the speedboat just when it was docking alongside the tug. The Coast Guard was contacted next, because they already had units patrolling the area. That's it!"

"Amazing!" Olivia breathed.

"And they caught Alex before she could put the replacement part in the new sonar she was selling to the bad guys. That means whales' lives are going to be saved. All because of Bindy!" Ashley exclaimed. "Let's all celebrate Bindy, the hero!"

Looking a little sheepish, Steven said, "I apologize for not believing you at first, Bindy."

She raised her eyebrows. "Yeah, getting believed. That's always the hard part."

"You're right," Steven said, covering her hand with his. "Now I understand what it's like not to be trusted. When I tried to tell the police what you'd said, they just brushed me off. I knew what they were thinking—I was some kind of incompetent who couldn't keep track of a foster child. After all, I'd already been to them twice about you running away, Bindy."

"And then you called them with this wild story about your two children missing, too," Bindy said. "So they figured this guy's a nut case, trying to get some attention. Yeah, I've been there."

All of them fell silent, probably thinking about Bindy's problems with Cole. Ashley asked, "How'd you get them to listen to you, Dad?"

"I made them call Harvard Medical School for the necropsy report on the dead whale. That's when they started to pay attention."

"Yay!" Ashley cheered, clapping her hands. "What a smart dad I have!"

Steven still looked a bit unhappy, and Jack wondered whether he was regretting all those great pictures he didn't get to take of Spud returning to the ocean. Maybe Olivia was thinking the same thing, because she said, "I know Steven's whale rescue photographs would have been the best, but there was plenty of media coverage about Spud. As the day went on, all the television stations for hundreds of miles around sent reporters and cameramen. The whole rescue is on videotape, so you kids will get to see Spud swimming back to his mamma."

"And you'll see me, too," Bindy said.

"What? Swimming back to your mamma?" Jack was trying to be funny, but as soon as he said it he wished he could bite his tongue. Bindy looked crestfallen.

"No. I meant I was on camera. Three of the TV reporters interviewed me about how I got you two rescued." Suddenly she brightened. "You know what? I *liked* being back on camera. I decided I really miss it."

Olivia nodded. "I can understand that, Bindy. You're a natural-born actress."

#

The stone steps leading down to Thunder Hole were slick with seawater. Careful to keep his hand on the railing, Jack could feel the condensation as he slid his palm down the cool metal. Since his parents had run into Greg in the parking lot, they'd told the kids to go on ahead to Thunder Hole, promising to catch up soon.

Before they left, Greg asked, "You kids know much about Thunder Hole?"

The three of them shook their heads no.

"It's a true natural wonder. Every once in a while a really big wave hits, and the force of it smacking the air inside the hollow cavern creates a clap so loud it's almost like a sonic boom. But it gets cold down there," he warned them. "Thunder Hole sprays out a lot of water, and with the breeze up like it is now, well, you'll feel the chill. You might want to grab your jackets."

"We didn't bring any," Ashley told him.

Olivia brightened. "Bindy, why don't you get those blankets we're going to return to the rangers? I left them in the car."

"Sure thing," Bindy answered, backtracking quickly.

Now, as the three of them made their way down the steps, Bindy threw one of the blankets around her shoulders while Ashley draped a second blanket over her head, clutching it under her chin. Jack had already decided that wearing a blanket would look too wimpy. He preferred to tough it out in his T-shirt.

The end of the pathway led to an enormous slab of rock enclosed by a steel railing. Its shape reminded Jack of the bow of a ship. Beneath him, he saw a natural cavern that had been carved, over eons, by the force of waves crashing against rock. The bullet-shaped hollow was deep enough that when the ocean rushed into it, water shot into the air like a geyser, before curling back on itself. As Jack leaned over the railing, a spent wave retreated; the blue-gray water roiled as if boiling in a cauldron.

"How come I don't hear anything but splashing?" Ashley asked. "Where's the boom?"

"Remember what Greg said. We have to wait for a really big wave before the sound happens. You have to be patient."

Another wave hit the hole, sending up a spray of water that seemed to burst into a million water crystals, but there was no boom. Jack watched the ocean, shivered, and waited. More swells hit Thunder Hole and retreated. A mist chilled his bare skin, and he could feel gooseflesh rising on his arms. Maybe he should have accepted a blanket.

Suddenly, Bindy grabbed Jack's arm. "Look! Here comes a huge one!" she cried, pointing. "Whoa—this ought to do it!"

He watched the line of a wave swell and curl, pushing toward the shore with mounting force until it hit the hole with tremendous power. A sound like thunder exploded around them, causing spray to shoot so high it seemed to touch the clouds. The water rained back down onto Thunder Hole before receding to the ocean once more. In the silence that followed, Jack heard droplets drizzle off the rocks in tiny waterfalls. "Man, that explosion sounded like a cannon," he exclaimed. "It was *loud!*"

"Hence, the name," Bindy told him, grinning. Pulling the blanket around her, she squinted into the sea, the wind tousling her hair into languid wisps. She seemed to be thinking about something.

"Hey, Bindy," Ashley commented, "what's wrong? It's like you got sad all of a sudden."

"I'm not sad. It's just—oh, I don't know. I was looking out there in the ocean for Spud and his mamma, hoping the two of them would be all right. I guess that made me think of my own mom. I...I miss her. So much." A flush crept across her cheeks, and Jack could hear her voice tighten. "Sometimes I'm OK, and then I see real families and I feel so *cheated*. It's not fair. None of it's fair."

Ashley moved closer, huddling against Bindy. "I heard that you got a call from your aunt today. Dad told me."

"Yeah." Bindy's face contorted. "So?"

In a voice barely heard above the waves, Ashley asked, "Is everything all right?"

Bindy shrugged. "Everything's fine. Couldn't be better." She pulled a strand of hair from her mouth, then looked back at the sea. Neither Jack nor Ashley said a word. Another huge wave rolled in, exploding into Thunder Hole and then showering the rocks in a furious torrent. After what felt like forever, Bindy finally spoke. "I might as well tell you what happened. I didn't tell your folks because I didn't feel like talking about it, but...." She took a deep breath. "Cole got into more trouble."

Jack leaned forward, alert. "What trouble?"

"I don't know all the details. I guess he beat up some player after a soccer game the other team won. This time a coach caught him doing it. Cole outweighed the other guy by about 60 pounds and hurt him pretty bad."

"Wow!" Jack breathed.

"Aunt Marian told me Cole has to go for psychological counseling. It's like a court order or something." Bindy frowned. "Cole tried to lie his way out of it, but when the coach told him he might lose his scholarship if he didn't complete the counseling, he broke down and confessed everything. He even told the coach how he used to hit me."

Ashley touched Bindy's arm and said, "That's good, isn't it?"

Waving her off, Bindy answered, "So now Cole's in this anger management class and Aunt Marian said...." She swallowed, then went on, "She said she...she wants me back. She said she realized she was wrong. She promised that Cole will be better now." Bindy laughed, but it wasn't a happy sound. "Like that fixes everything. All of a sudden I'm supposed to be grateful when she tells me she *understands* now. The part I don't get is—" Her eyes filled with tears as she wailed, "Why wouldn't she *believe* me to begin with? I told her what happened—I told her and told her and told her. How come my words weren't good enough? Why wasn't *I* good enough?"

Jack didn't know what to say. Bindy was right—what happened to her wasn't fair. But one thing he learned about having foster kids in his home was that sometimes bad things happened and there was no justice to it, but in the end you just had to go on, somehow. He rubbed his arms and searched for something to say, but everything that came into his mind sounded hollow, even to him.

Quietly, Ashley said, "You know, Bindy, when you were talking about Spud, I thought of a story I heard. Its an Inuit legend. Would you like to hear it?"

"I thought I was supposed to be the performing artist," Bindy said. "But go ahead, Ashley. Tell your story."

Pulling her blanket tightly around her shoulders, Ashley closed her eyes and began.

Many, many years ago, when the Earth was born, the Great Spirit created the land. Everything he made was good—he placed the sun in the sky to give warmth by day and the moon in the heavens to give light by night. He placed fish in the sea and filled the air with every kind of bird. He made the great bear, and the walrus, and the seal. Then, the Great Spirit made the Inuit people. And because the Great Spirit had a special love for the Inuit people, he became their teacher, showing them how to live by using everything around them.

Then the Great Spirit decided to make one thing more, the very best of his creation—the bowhead whale. This was his most beautiful creature. He gave it a song, and as it sailed though the waters, sharing its melody, the whale was in perfect balance with all of creation.

But the Great Spirit saw something else. His people needed the whale to survive the bitter-cold winters. With-out the muktuk, *the flesh of the whale, the people could not stay warm and healthy during the frigid nights. They needed the bones of the whale to create their homes. In short, they needed every part of the bowhead whale in order to live.*

And so the Great Spirit gave the bowhead to the Inuit.

With spring comes the thaw. The ocean ice breaks apart, creating a water road called the Open Lead. It is on the Open Lead that the bowheads swim, right into the harpoons of the Inuit. Every year the whales sing, and every year they come, waiting patiently for their death.

But, the Great Spirit decided this also. At the same time every year, when the Open Lead is formed, the Great Spirit sends a cloud of heavy mist to hover just above the ice, above the whales, and above the Inuit. The heavy cloud hangs in the air between the sky and the sea.

"Though I gave you permission to kill my most perfect creature, the whale," the Great Spirit said, "I do not wish to watch it happen."

Opening her eyes, Ashley searched Bindy's face.

"What are you trying to say?" Bindy asked. "Is that story supposed to mean something to me?"

Ashley nodded. "Maybe," she answered, "your aunt didn't want to believe what her son was doing, so she made a cloud to hide the truth. But now that she knows, she's trying to tell you she's sorry."

For a long moment Bindy stayed silent. Then she murmured, "Thanks, Ashley."

"Are you going to go back to her?"

"I don't know. Maybe. Maybe not." Turning to Jack, Bindy struggled to clear the emotion from her face. "You're wet. Look at you, you've got goose bumps all over. Here, take my blanket."

"I'm fine," Jack told her, shivering.

"No offense, but you've always been a bad actor. Come on, Jack-o, you're freezing. Take it!"

When he refused again, she said, "All right, then, we'll share. Ashley, you throw your blanket around him on one side, and I'll throw mine on the other, and if we huddle up together...." Jack felt himself enveloped in warm blankets. "Maybe we'll all survive."

Jack could hear Bindy's breathing, feel her rounded arm pressed against his, and on his other side he felt Ashley's knob of an elbow drill his ribs. They sat, the three of them, separate in their thoughts, yet united by what they'd been through together.

"We make a whale of a team," Bindy murmured.

She was right.

AFTERWORD

The evil scientist is caught. Jack, Bindy, and Ashley save the day, and Olivia and Steven save the whale. All is well. But while this story didn't actually happen, much of the details are based on fact. There are some important themes in *Out of the Deep* that are worth returning to.

First, it is important to understand there are two types of whales—those that have teeth and those that don't. Toothed whales (odontocetes) are typically smaller, and include dolphins, porpoises, beaked whales, sperm whales, and killer whales. Baleen whales (mysticetes) lack teeth. Instead they have rows of baleen plates that hang from the roof of the mouth. These plates strain microscopic food from the water. Common mysticetes include the humpback, fin, and minke whales.

Do whales really beach themselves? Yes, but not

frequently. In Maine, where Acadia National Park is situated, we respond to 5–10 toothed-whale strandings each year. Baleen-whale strandings are much rarer and happen perhaps once a year. In most cases the animal washes ashore already dead. Finding Spud alive in *Out of the Deep* meant people still had a chance to save him.

Why do whales strand? We really don't know. There probably isn't just one cause. In some cases whales may deliberately swim toward a beach and strand. If rescue teams are unable to re-float the whale and push it back to sea, then it will likely die of asphyxiation (meaning it will suffocate) or from massive internal trauma. Out of water, a whale cannot support its own weight. Gravity will crush its organs. In some cases, a whale will repeatedly strand. This apparently suicidal behavior is difficult to understand. Even more puzzling are mass strandings, in which several animals strand within a short period of time.

Scientists are careful to examine all possible causes of any kind of stranding. If a stranded whale dies, we quickly perform a necropsy to see if we can understand more about what happened. These examinations don't always answer our questions, as we still know very little about a whale's physiology. From personal experience I can tell you that performing a necropsy on an animal as large as a whale is a smelly and gory business, not for the faint of heart!

In this story, Olivia remembers a mass stranding that

actually happened in the Bahamas. Necropsies revealed that the ear structure in some of the whales had been destroyed. Eventually, the stranding was linked to local sonar testing by the Navy. I was one of the researchers at the Newfoundland stranding Greg mentions in the book. Examination of that humpback revealed that powerful sound waves had sheared the whale's earbone. That investigation was one of the first to suggest that exposure to loud sound could lead to a whale's death.

You may be wondering how sound can be so deadly to a whale. The answer lies in the way these animals perceive their world.

Think for a moment about how you take in the space around you. Vision is the sense we humans rely on most. This is because the air that surrounds us is transparent. But whales live in a watery environment where vision, at best, can only be used at short range. (Picture how far you can see underwater, even if you wear a mask and snorkel.) In contrast, sound travels very long distances in water—much farther than it does in air. Whales most likely "see" their surroundings as pictures painted not in color but in sound. When intense sound waves harm a whale's inner ear, they rob the animal of its ability to accurately sense its environment. It loses its ability to find its way.

Humans are but a small blip in the history of life on this planet. In contrast, whales have existed for about 60 million years. For most of that time, their environment was relatively quiet. But steadily over the past 200 years, humans have made the ocean a noisy place—first with the roar of boat engines, then with sonar and other types of sound devices. Whales have no way to protect themselves against this noise pollution. As a result, these magnificent animals have begun to suffer.

It is humbling to reflect upon how little we humans know about whales. We must learn about our impact on these mystical animals—not only about the effects of noise pollution or the use of sonar but also about the devastation of hunting that has brought many species to the brink of extinction. We must protect these creatures of the deep. Only knowledge combined with action ultimately will lead to a solution.

May it come in our lifetimes.

Sean Todd, Ph.D.
Professor, College of the Atlantic
Senior Researcher, Allied Whale
http://www.coa.edu/alliedwhale

DON'T MISS—

WOLF STALKER
MYSTERY #1
Fast-paced adventure has the Landons on the trail
of a wounded wolf in Yellowstone National Park.

CLIFF-HANGER
MYSTERY #2
Jack's desire to help the headstrong Lucky Deal
brings him face-to-face with a hungry cougar in
Mesa Verde National Park.

DEADLY WATERS
MYSTERY #3
Jack and Ashley's efforts to save an injured manatee
involve them in a thrilling chase through the Everglades.

RAGE OF FIRE
MYSTERY #4
In this tale of myth and mystery, a Vietnamese orphan
named Danny leads Ashley and Jack into a steaming
crater in Hawaii Volcanoes National Park.

THE HUNTED
MYSTERY #5
While attempting to help a young Mexican runaway, Jack
and Ashley flee for their lives from an enraged mother
grizzly in Glacier National Park.

GHOST HORSES
MYSTERY #6
Life-threatening accidents plague the Landons as they
investigate the mysterious deaths of some white mustangs
on a trip to Zion National Park.

OVER THE EDGE
MYSTERY #7
Jack relies on high-tech cyber skills to find out who is
threatening his mother after she broadcasts her plan to
save the condors in Grand Canyon National Park.

VALLEY OF DEATH
MYSTERY #8
A showdown with Ashley's kidnappers leads the Landons
to a missile testing ground and the key to what's killing the
desert bighorn sheep in Death Valley National Park.

ESCAPE FROM FEAR
MYSTERY #9
On a trip to Virgin Islands National Park to study sea turtles
and coral reefs, the Landons become entangled in a teenage
boy's desperate efforts to save the mysterious Cimmaron
from danger.

COMING SOON–

RUNNING SCARED
MYSTERY #11
While lost in a cave in Carlsbad Caverns National Park, the Landon
kids stumble on to some cave robbers and uncover a clue that helps
explain the park's dwindling bat population.

*To read samples from each of these mysteries,
go to Gloria Skurzynski's Web site:*
http://gloriabooks.com/national.html

ABOUT THE AUTHORS

An award-winning mystery writer and an award-winning science writer—who are also mother and daughter—are working together on Mysteries in Our National Parks!

Alane (Lanie) Ferguson's first mystery, *Show Me the Evidence,* won the Edgar Award, given by the Mystery Writers of America.

Gloria Skurzynski's *Almost the Real Thing* won the American Institute of Physics Science Writing Award.

Lanie lives in Elizabeth, Colorado. Gloria lives in Boise, Idaho. To work together on a novel, they connect by phone, fax, and e-mail and "often forget which one of us wrote a particular line."

Gloria's e-mail: gloriabooks@qwest.net
Her Web site: http://gloriabooks.com
Lanie's e-mail: aferguson@sprynet.com
Her Web site: http://alaneferguson.com